Your Book
of Shadows

Your Book of Shadows

How to Write Your Own Magickal Spells

✦ ✦ ✦ ✦ ✦ ✦ ✦ ✦ ✦ ✦ ✦

Patricia Telesco

CITADEL PRESS
Kensington Publishing Corp.
www.kensingtonbooks.com

CITADEL PRESS books are published by

Kensington Publishing Corp.
850 Third Avenue
New York, NY 10022

All Kensington titles, imprints, and distributed lines are available at special quantity discounts for bulk purchases for sales promotions, premiums, fund-raising, educational, or institutional use. Special book excerpts or customized printings can also be created to fit specific needs. For details, write or phone the office of the Kensington special sales manager: Kensington Publishing Corp., 850 Third Avenue, New York, NY 10022, attn: Special Sales Department, phone 1-800-221-2647.

First Kensington printing August 2001

10   9   8   7   6

Printed in the United States of America

Cataloging data for this title may be obtained from the Library of Congress.

ISBN 0-8065-2071-X

For everyone who realizes that a little Witch lives within, and wants to express that without, but has no idea where to begin. May these pages be a source of inspiration and a genesis to your magical path.

Contents

Acknowledgments

My thanks to David, Blythe, Colleen, Sirona, Dorothy, and AJ, who have constantly listened to ideas, read drafts, offered ideas freely, and generally kept me sane.

Also for my children and husband, who do everything possible to keep me crazy.

Introduction

Wizards and witches throughout history have valued their spellbooks. Far more than a simple compilation of mystical recipes for love, health, prosperity, and other daily needs, the spellbook preserved tradition, assembled personal insights, provided instructions, and collected good advice into one neat package. In other words, a good spellbook included everything necessary to walk the Path of Beauty wisely, skillfully, and confidently.

So why do many ancient spellbooks seem so enigmatic and distasteful? For several reasons. First, bear in mind the time periods during which these spellbooks originated. During those years, many of the supposed magical accounts were written by people seeking to destroy Wiccan beliefs. These people would "make up" spells and rituals that talked of heinous procedures to scare the public and provide ammunition for ostracization.

Second, many occult practitioners in the past believed that there was a limited amount of energy available to them. So, if a lot of people worked magic, there would be less power in it. In an effort to avoid this problem, they safeguarded basic procedures by hiding them in nonsense words and actions that had little meaning to the uninitiated, or someone who didn't understand the writer's code.

In the modern world things have made a wonderful change for the better. Many Wiccans and Pagans have come out of the prover-bial broom closet and begun sharing from their personal path or cultural traditions. In the process, we have started to rebuild our sacred books, assembling Books of Shadows that reveal the essence of Wiccans as they live and worship in today's reality.

Why do we call it a Book of Shadows? Because magical energy works between this world and the next, between sounds and silence, between the light and darkness. This power flows through the shad-ows, marking the border between what we know and the infinite possibilities of the universe. Somewhere at the meeting grounds of yesterday and forever, we find the spark of magic, then translate that experience and energy into written word as best we can.

This book is dedicated to helping you find that spark and inter-pret it suitably in your own path and vision. These pages act as a step-by-step guide to creating a personal Book of Shadows that will grow and change with you and your spiritual quest. It starts, in Part I, with an explanation of some of the mediums you can use to create your book, both simple and sublime. This section also provides instructions on making an effective spiritual space in which to work on your book, and how to bless the pages once they're completed.

Part II goes on to discuss thirteen potential sections that estab-lish the main body of your spellbook. These are guidelines only, but they're a good place to start. In my fourteen years of practice, I've noticed that people need a certain amount of "basic data" for casting successful spells, designing effective meditations, enacting potent rituals, and for generally understanding the modern magi-cal life. These thirteen sections contain as much of those basics as I could squeeze into one book without reaching critical mass.

Finally, Part III talks about the usefulness of keeping one part of your Book of Shadows set aside for reflections—a magical diary of sorts where you will write about things that touch you, things you're feeling, fresh insights, motivational ideas, and the like. You can read these pages and see concrete evidence of how much you're growing as a spiritual being. You'll also often find ideas here that will help you with many magical and mundane procedures and situations in the future.

Throughout this book I will be sharing excerpts from my own Book of Shadows and those from friends who have kindly given me permission to share the methods that they have found. You can use these to begin your own book, or adapt them as desired. See, this process requires that you follow your heart: magic begins with our will and desire, but it's guided by vision. So, think of this book like a black-and-white outline to which you bring the crayons of insight and imagination to design a Book of Shadows that is completely right for your magical path.

In some ways your Book of Shadows will never be "done" because magic is a lifelong journey that continually awakens and augments our spiritual nature. Even so, once you have the basics of your spellbook completed, it will be something you return to again and again for help and inspiration. Your Book of Shadows will also be a tome that you'll want to share, in part, with close friends and people of a like mind. Sharing what we've learned or discovered builds respect for various paths, helps internalize the lessons you're talking about, and encourages an open exchange of ideas from which everyone benefits.

So, sit down with me now in my figurative family room created in this book's pages, and read. By the time you're done with *Your Book of Shadows*, you'll have developed a very special magical book all your own—a book to be proud of, and one to treasure for many years to come.

PART I

Your Path, Your Power

I'm really glad you came here to work with me on your Book of Shadows. This is an effort that will benefit greatly from reading books and talking things through with people you respect. But before we really get down to creating your spellbook, you need a clear idea of what you want out of magic and your spiritual path.

See, in many ways your Book of Shadows acts as a magical diary. It's very intimate and reflective of all that you are, and all that you can be. This isn't just on a spiritual level either! The ancient Witches recognized that magic had to work hand in hand with everyday life for the most personally pleasing, most powerful, and most positive results. So, your Book of Shadows is going to have parts about your magical tradition, parts about your daily reality, and parts about how to blend these two seemingly conflicting things together. You simply can't do this if you have no idea about what kind of magic is right for you.

Mapping Your Magical Path

So where do you begin? For those reading this who have already carved out a personal path, just skip the next few paragraphs and go on to Modes and Mediums. For those who are uncertain as to what metaphysical/cultural tradition is right, please read this section carefully as it will influence how successful you'll be in making a spellbook that remains satisfying and fulfilling as time goes on.

In picking out a direction to follow for your path, you need to think about who you are as a person and what affects you deeply. Are you the "wing it" type? Do you prefer details and planning? Are you drawn to a particular cultural heritage? In answering these three questions you'll uncover the first street signs for mapping your magical path.

A person who prefers to wing it will likely find folk magic very satisfying because it's more flexible and adaptable to a variety of situations. Those who find detail and planning an effective coping mechanism for daily living will probably be more comfortable with High Magic, or ritualistic forms that have more structure. And, if you have a particular culture that attracts your interest (like Greek, Egyptian, Celtic, etc.) then you can add that cultural flavor to whichever form of magic you've chosen!

I should mention at this point that you can certainly mix and mingle good ideas and techniques from folk magic and ritual magic together. You can also blend a variety of culturally specific concepts to create an eclectic system all your own. At this point, however, all you're trying to do is find a focal point from which to start the mapping process. Where you take your Book of Shadows from there is really up to you! So take a moment now to think very seriously about the questions I've posed, and the metaphysical tradition that intrigues you the most and make that your map's key.

By the way, where you begin your magical map, and where you end up a few years down the road, can be two very different places. Wicca as a belief system grows and changes with you and the Earth, so what's "right" for you spiritually will also transform. This means that periodically you'll have to revamp your Book of Shadows accordingly.

Confused yet? I know I was fifteen years ago when someone first told me all this, but with time and effort it all starts making sense.

Read as much as you can, talk to as many people in the magical community as you can, meditate, pray, and trust your heart. Even with all that, you probably won't discover the perfect magical approaches right away—that usually happens with trial and error.

Simply apply an enthusiastic spirit and firm will, and you'll get where you want to be both magically and mundanely. Just be patient and try to remember that spirituality doesn't require keeping up with a pace set by someone else, or even with a pace you might wish you could maintain! Your soul will grow in its own time and in its own way, and so will your Book of Shadows.

Modes and Mediums

Once you've figured out what route to take, you can start paying attention to other details. Every skilled mapmaker has to consider how the finished creation will be used, what medium or mediums best represent that application, and what inks, colors, and scale should be used. All of these considerations apply to your Book of Shadows too!

Begin by taking into account your time constraints and your talents. Do you have the time it takes to make an elaborate book, or do you need something simpler and more adaptable? Do you enjoy hand crafts, or are you like me—someone who was born "all thumbs"? These two simple questions will help you decide what base medium is best for your Book of Shadows. Those who need something simple and adaptable will want to begin with a three-ring binder, a prefabricated bound diary, or the blank lined pages of this book and a variety of colored pens. Those who have more artistic tendencies can consider making their own paper, using calligraphy pens, paints, making a special decoupage cover, or whatever.

Please know that neither approach is right or wrong. Part of living the magical life is recognizing both our talents and limitations, and then working within that structure to the best of our ability. For example, all my publishers know that I cannot draw—everything tends to look like the scribbles made by my four-year-old! I try to draw with my words instead, and fill those with the creative energy that other people put into their handcrafts. You can do likewise.

Even the simplest medium, the three-ring binder, can be made special. For example:

- Photocopy a goddess image and glue it to the cover using an all-purpose adhesive blended with magical herbs like powdered frankincense.
- Cut out inspiring images from magazines and pattern them on the cover so they create a pentagram (sketch out the star first and then glue images at each point). Use any elemental symbols that occur in the images to determine their placement (like a seashell in the western area of the pattern, and a candle in the southern area).
- Simpler still, just use a large, lovely font on your computer and type up a cover. Dab this with some personally significant oil to mark it as your own.

See, the base medium for your Book of Shadows need not be elaborate to be *meaningful,* and in magic *meaning* is *everything!* Whatever you decide to do, however, I recommend finding a way to do it yourself. While it's nice to have talented people make things for us, your Book of Shadows should bear your energy signature from beginning to end. Even when you write down something shared from a friend, it's YOU writing it, and therefore your vibrations go into the pages.

Here are some ideas and instructions for ways that you can individualize your spellbook to make it more visually appealing, personally significant, and magically potent:

Homemade Paper

Making homemade paper is messy but fun. It's also something anyone can learn to do. For the basic process you will need a bundle of scrap paper equal in mass to two full newspaper pages. You can use junk mail, magazines, construction paper, left over newspapers, and the like to make your paper, and you'll be recycling in the process! You will also need:

a blender or food processor
2 tbs. white glue
2.5 cups of water
sink filled with 4″ of water
old pantyhose and coat hanger (or framed screening)
iron

OPTIONAL ADDITIVES   These are put into the mixture after you've made the pulp for your paper

food coloring
essential oil
dryer lint
confetti or feathers
sequins or glitter
threads or lace
cut up bits of ribbon or colored paper
finely ground or diced dried herbs, flower petals, fruit fibers, or
    vegetable pieces
tea leaves or coffee grounds

THE PROCESS   If possible, choose a time and date that will benefit the type of energy with which you're saturating the paper. For example, wait until a full moon to make the paper for the personal insight section of the magical diary. Or, wait until a waning moon to make the paper that will be used for banishing spells.

Next, take the coat hanger or another long piece of sturdy wire and bend it into a frame. The size of the frame should be equal to the size you want your paper to be when completed. While a square or rectangle shape is customary, you can change the shape if you wish as long as you have a way to safeguard the paper afterward. To illustrate: make round paper for sacred circle notes, then place them between cloth-covered cardboard that you lace together.

Stretch the hose over the frame so it's flat and secure. Or, use framed screening like that for a door. I suggest making several frames so you can create more than one piece of paper at a time without a waiting period in between.

Once the frames are put together, get the blender out (or a food processor). Put one-third of your scrap paper into the blender with a little bit of water. Use the high setting. Slowly add the rest of the paper and water until it's completely incorporated. At this point, run the blender for two to three more minutes. If you want to add any of the optional ingredients that provide texture and/or darker colors, do so now and mix it by hand until the chosen substance is equally dispersed.

For the spiritual dimension, make sure that the colors, herbs, or other additives match the theme presented by a particular part of your Book of Shadows. For example, add powdered or dried rose petals and other pinkish-red ingredients for the page that will contain love spells, or add lettuce, ginger powder, and orange peel to the batch of paper intended for prosperity rituals.

Put your frames in the bottom of the sink filled with water. If you want to add food coloring (which makes a faintly tinted paper) or scents, this is the time to do so. As before, match the colors and aromas to your magical purpose, like lavender oil and blue food coloring for pages dealing with peace and forgiveness. Sprinkle the food coloring (or plant juice) and essential oil into the water, then pour your paper into the sink water, add the glue, and mix them together. For best results, pretend you're kneading bread. Now, take the frame and slowly lift it through the water so it collects an even covering of paper fiber. Do this with each frame until all your paper pulp is used up. If you run out of frames and have leftover pulp, this can be frozen or stored for up to a week in your refrigerator and used again in your next batch.

Each frame has to dry completely. You can set them in a warm window, hang them off the clothesline, or whatever. When dry, the paper will peel away easily and you can reuse the frame for more sheets. Put the completed sheet on the ironing board with a cloth underneath it and iron using the high setting. This removes the last bits of water from the paper. Let it dry again for at least forty-eight hours before using.

When cleaning up from this effort, I highly recommend taking the remnants outside or flushing them down the toilet a little at a time. Gather up the sink water and paper using a large cup or ladle and put it in a bucket with the wash water for the blender and dispose of it. The mixture tends to clog drains badly.

Note: If you don't have time to go through this process, it's not difficult to find really lovely stationery and paper products at a good office supply store or gift shop. You can scent this paper pretty easily by putting it in a box that's been dabbed with essential oil. The paper will usually absorb the aroma in a few weeks. If not, dab a little oil directly on the paper's corners. This last method is especially effective with spell papers that you plan to burn as components—the flame releases the oil's aroma and carries your magic to the heavens and across the land!

Unique Inks

If you'd like to make your own ink for your Book of Shadows out of natural materials, it's not as hard as you might expect. The Native Americans often used the juice of pokeweed for ink, while Europeans decocted elderberries, hollyhock, and sloes. Or, for a really neat twist you can write secret or highly private parts of your spellbook-diary in vinegar, lemon juice, or onion juice. These three mediums dry invisibly. The text can then only be read by holding the paper in front of a light source (for magic, I suggest a candle).

To scent inks, simply add about ten drops of essential oil to a small bottle of ink and label it. You have to find a pen that can accept the ink from a well to use this, but it's worth it. The scent adds extra symbolism and even acts as subtle aromatherapy whenever you're reading that section!

Drawings/Photographs

Adding imagery to your pages gives your magical purpose a visual form. Even if the drawing is simple, like that of a rune that corresponds to the page's theme, it provides one more dimension to the energy you're creating. Every sensual cue you give yourself (visual, tactile, etc.) improves the overall impact of the page on your superconscious self. In other words, these extra touches help you internalize what you're writing in your spellbook on a more intimate and spiritual level.

Note that if you use graphite or colored pencil drawings you can fix the image by dipping the pencil in skim milk and lightly painting the image with it afterwards. This is a nice alternative to using chemically based sprays.

Pressed Flowers and Herbs

There is nothing more whimsical than opening the pages of a book and discovering a perfectly preserved blossom inside. Better still, if the flower or herb resting on the page of your spellbook represents the section theme, you'll have a handy, dry, energized spell component at the ready!

To press flowers or herbs, try and choose ones that are already somewhat flat. Pick them when they're dry, and use a soft toothbrush to clean off any residual dirt. Place your chosen herbs and flowers on a large piece of absorbent paper. Space them out so there's about an inch between each item. Put several paper towels on top, then another sheet of absorbent paper (like the paper grocery bags are made from), and more flowers and herbs.

You can assemble up to one inch of material in this manner, hen lay several heavy books or slabs of wood on top. It will take about six weeks for the greenery to dry and press completely. The greenery should peel off easily and not feel the least bit damp when you check the layers. If it seems damp, wait another week. Then use them in your spellbook to give more significance to the words. Glue a bay leaf next to the spell for strength, a marigold next to your pre-bedtime ritual for receiving prophetic dreams, and so forth. Let the citizens of nature adorn your Book of Shadows and your magic in meaningful, lovely ways.

Book Covers

Earlier this chapter I made some suggestions for simple book covers. Alternatives to this exist, including looking into bookbinders in your area. Many will create custom book covers to your specifications for under $75 (this price usually includes some fine tooling, fancy lettering, and hinge work). A less expensive approach is to buy everything you need at a leather working shop and get some instructions from the salespeople. Making a book cover this way is kind of fun because you can design a look that makes it appear like the tome is hundreds of years old, right off a mage's shelf!

A third version is a little less complex than working in leather, but looks quite impressive when done. Take a piece of fabric large enough to cover your binder or diary, and make a small pocket on the inside. To measure, lay out the fabric and lay the open book flat on top. Cut an excess of one inch above and below the book, and at least four inches to the right and left (note that at least one inch of this gets taken up when you close the book).

Next, from the top of the fabric, fold over one-fourth inch two times and stitch it down (this creates a finished edge). Repeat this on the bottom. Fold down the top and bottom again another one-half inch and iron it in place. Lay this on the table with your book on top. If you've done this first part correctly, the top and bottom of the fabric are now even with the outside of the top and bottom of your spellbook's cover.

The second phase is a little easier. Slide the front cover into the pocket created by the folds of fabric at the top and bottom. Do the same with the back cover. Close the book and stitch the inner fold to the outside cloth (this will leave some strands of thread going over the edge of the book cover). This way when the cloth gets soiled you can simply snip those strands, remove the cover, and wash it. From here you can do a lot of things to customize the cloth. You could add a small pocket on top of the front cover into which you can put magically charged herbs. Or, glue on some crystal cabochons in a pattern that pleases both your eyes and spirit.

One of the neatest covers I ever saw incorporated a mirror that was held in place by quilted fabric. This idea comes from the old story about the seeker who looked the world over for the secrets of enlightenment. Finally she found herself atop a high mountain staring at a sacred book. Excited, her heart pounding, the person opened the book to discover a mirror. The secrets of enlightenment and real magic are always inside us—we just have to look!

Color Symbolism

Psychology has shown us that colors can drastically influence human behaviors and emotions. If you don't think this is true, just watch the difference in energy levels between when you're in a brightly colored room and when you're in a dark area for the same amount of time. Wiccans and many other metaphysical practitioners use the effects of color to empower their techniques and add more symbolic dimensions to various procedures.

Each color has specific magical associations that have been used for hundreds of years. You can use these same associations to energize and augment your Book of Shadows. Do this by carefully considering the colors you choose for your paper, ink, book cover, drawings, pressed flowers, etc. For a list of general correspondences to get you started, refer to Part II and the Color, Sound, and Texture section.

Mind you, if, because of personal experience, a color has a different meaning for you than what I provide, always go with your first impressions. It's not necessary that anyone else understand the "whys" of how you assemble your spellbook, and it's completely unnecessary to allow any book (or person) to dictate this creative, intuitive process. What's important is that *you* know why, and put some sincere thought into the whole process.

Paint

If you decide to use paint to adorn your spellbook in any way, I suggest choosing a nontoxic variety. Why? Because toxicity has a generally negative affect on magical energy (By the way: this is why so many people suggest using nonchemical sources for lighting ritual fires). Additionally, for individuals with pets or children, the rule "safety first" definitely applies. Go with what's safe so you can focus on the energy you're creating instead of worrying that your base materials might get into the wrong hands.

Calligraphy or Special Fonts

Starter calligraphy sets are readily available in many gift shops today, including the larger bookstores. Mind you, if you're a beginner I'd practice a bit before trying your hand on the pages of your spellbook. The more adept calligrapher can look through the various styles available and choose one whose visual personality best suits the overall look of the tome. For example, someone who has made an elaborate leather cover with brass hinges and a lock might want to use a medieval-styled script, akin to those found in monastic books of the Dark Ages. Someone who has chosen a Victorian theme might want to try a precise yet flowery style as was seen in many period signatures.

For people like me who tend to leave globs of ink behind while attempting such an endeavor, the wonderful world of technology offers a simpler alternative: computer fonts. You can look at either the name of the font, its visual impact, or both, to make a decision here. For example, Albertus or Letter Gothic might be suited to an antique-looking spellbook, while Univers is good for more contemporary styles or perhaps for spells designed to increase your "Univers-al" awareness!

Bad puns aside, you can also use different styles of fonts to emphasize various parts of your text. For example, use bold lettering for things that you want to draw your attention, or use the strikeout function as part of a banishing spell. Progressively larger lettering would be neat in a ritual or spell designed for increasing anything, while subscript and other tiny prints emphasize diminishing. Italics work wonderfully to show that someone in particular is speaking in a procedure, such as the High Priest/Priestess in a ritual.

For those of you looking for some good font options, check out Adobe Type manager and the Windows 95 font manager. These have a tremendous variety from which to choose. Also, people making more modern looking spellbooks might want to review the *Star Trek* fonts, or other similar popular media for ideas.

Scent-ual Appeal

The reemerging art of aromatherapy is thousands of years old. Texts dating to at least 1500 B.C.E. reveal the use of various aromatics to make people feel better or as suitable offerings to the god/dess. For example, lavender was often recommended for melancholy and it also appeared on numerous altars around the world to please the divine.

If you'd like to use scented paper or inks to symbolically accent segments of your Book of Shadows, here's a brief correspondence list to which to refer. You may, at some point, want to add this list to your spellbook, adding to it any new correspondences you find along with any personal meanings:

MAGICAL AROMATIC ATTRIBUTES OF OILS

Cedar   courage, strength, purification
Chamomile   peace, tranquility, healing
Coriander   energy (improving)
Geranium   balance, symmetry, harmony
Ginger   power
Jasmine   socialization
Lavender   peacefulness, sleep, lifting despair
Mint   prosperity
Myrrh   meditations, protection
Orange Bergamot   soothing anxiety
Rose   love (can change with color of the flower used)
Rosemary   memory, healing, hex breaking
Sage   psychic, astral purification, turning negativity
Sandalwood   spirituality, psychism
Vanilla   passion
Vetiver   change, shape shifting, glamoury
Violet   wellness, protection

If you have the time, I suggest making your own herbal oils from scratch so they're saturated with intention. The fastest way of making oils is to find a good quality base, like almond oil, and warming it in a non-aluminum pan. Steep your chosen herb (or a blend) in the oil until it takes on a tea-like quality. Repeat as often as necessary with fresh herbs to achieve the desired strength.

Note that it's vitally important that the oil you use is warm, not hot. Certain herbs, flower petals in particular, don't take well to high temperatures. Steeping them in very hot oil results in a nasty aroma similar to what old, moldy plants smell like. So take your time here, and consider working during an auspicious astrological phase to improve the results, like working during a full moon to encourage a fullness of love.

Also note that hard or dense plant matter like roots, seeds, and barks should be sliced thinly, ground, or bruised to release their aroma and energy more effectively. Berries can be mashed to give the oil a color symbolism as well as aroma; certain flower petals have this effect too. For best results, pick your flowers early in the morning before the sun dries them out.

Strain the oil using cheesecloth or an old set of stockings, and dispose of the herb remnants. Store the oil in a dark, air-tight container in a cool area to increase longevity. Label the jar listing the ingredients used, your magical intention, and any symbolic timing you used in the creation process. If at any time you notice that the oil has grown cloudy or taken on a repugnant scent, dispose of it. This means the oil has gone bad, and when that occurs the magical energy dissipates. So, the fresher

---

Hint: Herbal oils are useful for many magical efforts including:

- Anointing your chakras to open the path for specific energies
- Mingling with dried wood powder to make empowered incense
- Dabbing on light bulbs or candles to fill a room with magic
- Adding to bath water to change your auric vibrations
- Diluting with mineral oil for a magically-charged massage
- Polishing wooden wands to keep them from cracking and buffing in more positive energy in the process

the oil, the fresher the magic! Most oils created this way last six months to a year.

Wax Works

For hundreds of years, in a variety of cultures, wax was favored as a way of leaving one's personal mark on letters or other important documents. Signet rings were made specifically so a person could press them into wax, and seal his or her words safely within. Anyone receiving this paper would know immediately by its wax impression from whom the message came.

Since your Book of Shadows is definitely among the most important documents in your life, you might want to mark its pages similarly. This can be accomplished by purchasing a wax sealing kit at a stationery store, choosing the kit according to the impression that it makes. Some have initials, some have flowers, and there are a few other designs out there.

If you're feeling creative, however, you might want to try making your own wax imprint using soapstone, which is a very soft medium for carving. I get mine nearby in the Asian district of Toronto, at Eastern import stores, or through geology shows. The first two places might offer to carve an image that you want in the stone, saving you considerable time and the errors that naturally come with trying a new art. If they don't, then you'll need some small knives and files to do it yourself.

Trace the desired pattern on a flat side of the stone. If the piece you've obtained has no workable flat surfaces, sand a side flat. Slowly start carving out the image by digging gently into the stone with the tip of a file or knife along the outline. Repeat this procedure, progressively making the carved out portion a little deeper and wider with each repetition. This is necessary to ensure that the image will leave an impression in cooling wax. Don't go too quickly or you're likely to break off more than you want or crack the stone.

I should note at this point that it is possible to carve the entire stone in a similar manner using knives, files, and sandpaper. If you plan on carving the base of the wax seal into a particular shape or image, you should do this *before* fashioning the wax seal pattern on the bottom. Why? Because, from experience I can tell you, carving the base will often leave scratches on the flat bottom surface that you'll have to sand out in order to finish your sealing image. Also, the base carving sometimes breaks the stone along a fault line, leaving you with less of a wax sealing surface than anticipated.

When you think you're done with both the base and the wax imprint, test your work by putting a few drops of wax on a piece of paper and letting it cool slightly. Press the carved soapstone surface evenly into the wax. If the image isn't what you wanted, or not defined enough, you now have something to look at when making finishing touches in the carving. Should any wax adhere to the soapstone, you can get it off by dipping the soapstone in boiling water.

When your carving is completed and you're happy with the image it makes, follow this procedure to increase the seal's longevity. Preheat your oven to two hundred degrees and put the stone in it to warm for a half hour. Take it out using a good pot holder and slowly rub regular candle wax into the hot stone. When you get to the part where you did the carving, try to keep the wax on the flat surface only. This results in a nice, shiny finish and improves overall durability.

Odds 'n' Ends

Save bits of ribbon, glitter, those neat little stars and moons for inserting into greeting cards, buttons, silk flowers, tiny colored beans, fabric paint, small seashells or sand, minuscule stones with flat surfaces, evocative pictures from magazines and other media, feathers, mismatched jewelry, and the like. All of these things, and many more, can adorn your Book of Shadows when you're looking for something really different that also matches your goal perfectly. For example, dab the edges of a page that talks about fairies with watered-down glue, then sprinkle on glitter to look like fairy dust, or on a page about cooking magic, pattern some tiny dried beans to look like a spoon. Get creative and have a little fun!

Gathering Information

If you thought deciding between all the materials and mediums for assembling your Book of Shadows was difficult, it's only the beginning. Every step in assembling your spellbook will likely take similar serious thought and introspection. After all, what you put into this book both substantively and spiritually reflects who you are now and what you hope to be in the future. So, it's not something to slap together recklessly or without some consideration.

The next step in the process of creating your book is information gathering. Exactly where you find your information is up to you. Talk to people you respect and trust, look through well-documented books, watch educational tapes or programs on the Craft, make notes of your own personal experience and insights, take notes at gatherings you attend, and so forth. As you do, make sure to write down the source from which you received the information. There are several reasons for this:

You may want to go back to that source later for more insights or clarification.

You may want to recommend that source to someone else.

When writing an article or speaking about the subject, you'll want to be able to cite your resources.

If you integrate any materials into a public ritual or other public forums, copyright laws require proper acknowledgment.

At this stage of the game, I highly recommend drafting or writing up your notes in one place and transferring them into your formalized book later. Drafting the information gives you the chance to mull over several important questions including:

1. What parts of the assembled information do you feel are the most timeless and inspiring? These are the sections you'll want to give the most attention to when you transfer them into your spellbook (see the "Magical Work Room" section in this chapter).

2. What parts of the gathered information can you do without (in other words, it's not really reflective of your vision or your fla

vor of magic)? You can either throw these portions away or keep them in a separate file or binder. The advantage to the second option is having materials that offer "food for thought" for research or to get a different perspective.

3. What part of the information do you anticipate becoming quickly outdated? You probably want to keep this for a while in a three-ring binder so you can add in updates as necessary.

4. What parts of the material do you need to personalize, expand, shorten, or otherwise edit? Play around with these until they feel just right (but still keep a note of where the original concept came from).

5. What's the best way to present the materials you decide to keep in completed form? Do they need to be printed, written in calligraphy or typed? Should a specific color or aroma be added? Do you want to mix the information with art or illustrations?

6. How can you best organize this material? There's nothing more frustrating than needing information from your Book of Shadows and not remembering where you put it. So, carefully consider into which section of the book each piece of information should go, and if it should be repeated anywhere or cross-referenced.

You'll note from reading the last five points that your Book of Shadows may actually consist of several different books or sub-files. One book acts as the core of your faith. Another tome (or storage area) houses things that change quickly like popular books about magic, and yet another maintains information from other systems that you might want to use for comparative study or alternative outlooks.

Why bother with so many different types of storage? First, when you put a lot of work into a beautifully crafted spellbook, you don't want to be ripping or blotting sections out! Second, while a lot of things can be helpful to our arts, they're not always timely or practical. Your main spellbook should contain the ideas, methods, and correspondences that you need almost daily, not a lot of extraneous material. Having alternative places in which to store this extra material alleviates both problems.

Each edition of the spellbook can be maintained most easily on a computer disk. For those who don't have access to computers, try suitably labeled filling folders or small three-ring binders instead. Here are some of the alternatives you might want to have, other than those already cited:

- A table of contents and an index for ease of reference. This should give the page and edition location for each subject.
- Magical Artists: Musicians, writers, painters, etc. who really inspire you. These will change with the times and so it's best to keep the list separate or as a section in one of your secondary spellbook editions.
- Technomagic: Because technology is transforming faster than anyone can keep up with, this is definitely a section that will need regular updates and reformatting.
- Internet Resources: Along with technology, the Internet shifts and changes faster than most people change their socks. It's almost impossible to keep this data current, so store it where you can delete, add, and change listings frequently.
- Networking Contacts: We live in a very mobile society, so you'll probably want to keep your magical address book separate from the main text.
- Children's Rituals and Magical Projects: These come in very handy for groups with actively participating children. But not everyone has children, and those who do don't necessarily bring their children up in the Craft, so you might want this separate from your core information.
- Glossary of Terms: Word usage and meaning changes with the times quite rapidly, so keep this in a separate file.

I should probably mention at this point that the process of collecting, reviewing, editing, and transferring information into all of your spellbook's editions is ongoing. For as long as you practice magic you'll be stumbling across new ideas, new ways of approaching old issues, alternative techniques, creative adaptations, and the like that you'll want to keep and treasure. That's part of the wonder of magical traditions—they're like an ever-progressing kaleidoscope that shifts and transforms to continually amaze, teach, empower, and fulfill us.

Magical Work Room

Okay, you've figured out what materials and primary information to use for your Book of Shadows. But this isn't the kind of project that you can undertake when life all around you is chaotic and noisy. Being a kind of "bible" for the witch, the sacredness of the book is created in part by your attitude when putting it together, where you put it together, and when.

Attitude

Attitude is created cooperatively by your body, mind, and spirit. Physically you should be well rested and healthy. Mentally you should be alert, peaceful, and not carrying any grudges or negativity. Spiritually you should feel energized, psychically attuned, and purified so the energy that goes into your Book of Shadows is clean and unhindered.

I find one thing that helps people reach this balance is taking a special bath or shower beforehand. Begin by finding a set of clothes that you will wear *each time* you work on your spellbook, like a unique shirt that makes you feel magical, or perhaps a more traditional robe. (These can often be purchased at Pagan gatherings or over the Internet if you don't have a good seamstress to make one for you.) Take these with you to the bath or shower. Also prepare a bundle of cinnamon sticks (psychism and spirituality), lemon rind (purification), dried lavender (peace), thyme (health), and ginger (power) and place it in the hot bath water. In a shower this can be accomplished by hanging the bundle by a string from the showerhead.

Next, as you take off your present clothing, concentrate on removing worldly thoughts. Put aside your worries, situations from

the day, and the like. Focus your mind and heart on the project at hand. Breathe deeply of the aromas created by the herbs, and let their energies saturate your auric field. The water cleanses away any residual negativity, and it's also associated with the psychic self, so it's the perfect medium to put you in the right mood.

When you're done in the shower or bath, dress in the outfit you've picked out, symbolically adorning yourself with Spirit, then go right to work. You can easily shift back into normal awareness simply by changing back into the other set of clothing when you're done! If you repeat this procedure each time you work on your spellbook, it creates a mini-ritual that improves in meaning and power with each repetition.

If this particular approach doesn't make sense to you, try to find some type of pattern to follow that does. The pattern creates intention, and therefore a path for magical energy to follow. The pattern also prepares your mind and spirit for the task ahead, so any metaphysical endeavor will flow more easily.

Ambiance

Once you're prepared, the next step is to similarly ready the area in which you're planning to work. For a little while your kitchen, dining room table, or wherever, is going to become the focal point for designing your spellbook. So, you need to do some things to make that area look and feel different from the way it does normally. For one thing, put away any clutter (like a pile of bills or work related materials) that might easily distract you from your magical mind-set.

Next, think about any objects or items you have around that make you feel special in the spiritual sense. Crystals, a god or goddess statue, some fresh flowers, and the like, can be moved into your work area to create an ambiance suitable to your goal. To this basic foundation, you can make three more easy additions that can improve the overall impact of your magical work room. You will quickly see that the idea is to surround yourself with sights, sounds, and smells that kindle the fires of your spiritual-magical nature.

CANDLES The light of a candle represents the presence of the divine and the illumination you're ultimately hoping to find along your spiritual path. Better still, this is a magical tool that's very easy to make at home out of old candle ends and pieces, some essential oil, finely powdered herbs and flowers, and a tin or plastic container.

To begin, warm your wax in a double boiler. Remove any bits of wick that might be left behind if you're recycling old candle parts. Melt enough to fill whatever container you've chosen. Turn off the heat and let the wax cool just slightly before adding essential oil (to personal preference) or herbs and flowers. Meanwhile, lightly grease the inside of your container for ease of unmolding. Add a wick, which you can hang over the mouth of the chosen receptacle by tieing it to a pencil or chop stick. Consider weighing the bottom of the wick with a tiny crystal like a rose quartz to inspire self-love and positive energy. This will also serve a practical purpose, as it helps keep the wick in place while you pour the wax mixture into the mold. Let it cool and set completely. Remove the finished candle by warming the sides of the container with hot water.

By the way, make sure you match the oils, herbs, and/or flowers to your magical goals. For example, you could use the same blend in the candle as you use for your ritual shower by simply powdering some of the lemon rind and cinnamon before adding them to the melted wax. Then, when you light the candle in your work room it maintains a continuity of magical energy that began in the shower or bath and ends when you're done working on the spellbook for that day (by blowing out the candle)!

INCENSE   Incense has been an important ingredient in nearly all spiritual pursuits around the world. It was used to cleanse temples, as offerings to gods and goddesses, as a meditative tool, as a purification and a visionary tool in Native American traditions, and as a symbol of the prayers of the faithful rising to the heavens. With this in mind, a little incense (or potpourri for those with severe allergies) is the perfect tool for changing the vibrations in your magical work room.

Making incense isn't difficult, and I recommend using homemade over commercial blends because the store-bought kind often contains chemicals that negatively affect magical procedures. Some herbs, like dried lavender stems with heads, are nature-made incense sticks. These can be stuck in sand or dirt and simply lit to create an aroma.

For powdered incense you'll need to find a base of ground wood (pine, cedar, or sandalwood are recommended). I sometimes collect my wood powder at the homes of friends who have fireplaces. There's usually an abundance of tiny shards and fine powder left over from cutting up the timber. Pieces that are too large can be easily ground up using an old pencil sharpener, provided you slice them thinly!

Once you have about a cup of powdered wood, you can then add dried herbs, finely powdered flower petals, and essential oils to the mix. I don't recommend using much more than three or four additives at first until you know how they smell when burned. One blend to try, again, is the same one you use for your shower and candle! To one cup of sandalwood powder add two teaspoons powdered lemon rind, one teaspoon thyme, one teaspoon of ginger, and two of lavender. To improve the scent add essential oils (two drops per each should be sufficient). If you've added oils, you'll need to let the mixture dry before burning. Otherwise you can use it right away by sprinkling it on a fire source, like self-lighting charcoal and a good fireproof base.

MUSIC   The old saying that "music soothes the savage beast" has some bearing on creating an effective magical ambiance. In this case, the figurative beast to tame is your everyday life—all the hustle, bustle, noise, pressures, and responsibilities that barrage you every day. If you think of how you feel at the end of a rough day, you can see why it's important to shift your thoughts and awareness away from the material and toward more spiritual, tranquil topics before working on your spellbook. Music is one means of helping that process along.

With or without words, music has the unique capacity to touch us deeply—inspiring laughter or tears, and generally just reaching the core of what it is to be human. That includes your spiritual nature. So, ask some magical friends about the artists they personally prefer for meditation, circles, and other magical procedures. Borrow the compact disc or tape and see if it's something that ignites your soul. If so, go get a copy and play it while you work on your Book of Shadows.

Timing

The ancient mages often used timing as an ingredient in creating potent magic. The belief was (and still is) that the phases of the moon, positioning of the sun, and placement of the stars in the heavens all influence life on Earth in positive or negative ways. For example, whenever Mercury goes retrograde it seems that all forms of communication get messed up, and most magical practitioners just wait until this phase is over to approach any important exchange, be it written or verbal. So, I wouldn't suggest working on your spellbook during this time either!

To work on your Book of Shadows during an auspicious astrological time, here's what I recommend. *Hint:* you may want to add these associations to your spellbook in the section for "The Wheel of Life" under "timing."

- The month of May Emphasize personal growth, blossoming awareness, transformation, and awakening.
- The month of September Emphasize spirituality, especially development and maturity in this part of your life.
- The month of December Improve your understanding of the mysteries and universal truths.
- A waxing to full Moon Stress continued growth into a fullness of Be-ing. Note that the Moon is also strongly symbolic of the intuitive self, which is so necessary to magic.
- Moon in Cancer Support your desire for awareness, spiritual sensitivity, and the inventive nature.
- Moon in Libra Create a truly balanced Book of Shadows that's filled with keen perceptions.
- Moon in Capricorn For your magical diary especially this moon sign helps you see and express yourself truthfully, and develop the best of your inner attributes.
- Moon in Sagittarius This moon sign is goal oriented, so if you need a motivational nudge to get to work, this is a good choice.
- Wednesday Stressing the creative, innovative self in making your spellbook.
- Thursday Effectively communicate your ideas in your Book of Shadows.
- Sunday Improve your spiritual studies. (This isn't so much a time to work on the book as it is for reviewing what you've done so far.)

I've included more information about timing later in this book, but suffice it to say that timing magical work "perfectly" can become a somewhat arduous task considering all the different correspondences. I wouldn't get too hung up on this point. Simply keep it in mind for those occasions when you want extra cosmic energy working in your favor.

Sacred Space

Your magical work room can be any space so long as you can easily lay out all your materials and work in privacy. You should, however, seriously consider creating a protected magical sphere within which to accomplish your tasks. There are a couple of reasons for this. First, sacred space vibrates at a higher level and will help saturate your Book of Shadows with positive energy.

Second, spiritual entities are often drawn to magical work like bees to nectar. Not all of these entities are positive, and not all of them have your best interests at heart. Establishing sacred space eliminates that problem. It puts a spiritual shield between you and outside influences that could deter or detract you from what you're trying to accomplish. This spiritual shield doesn't just keep out distracting entities, it also stops negative energy originating from individuals or situations nearby.

In case you're not familiar with the basic procedure for activating a magic circle, here's one approach to try. Please change any wording that you feel uncomfortable with so that the invocation flows effortlessly from you to the Guardians and Spirit. Ultimately, a heartfelt prayer will bless and protect a space as well as any intricately contrived invocation.

SEVEN STEPS FOR CREATING SACRED SPACE

Hint: Transfer this to the ritual or sacred space section of your spellbook. You can adapt this particular invocation to many different magical pursuits simply by changing the wording.

1. Gather together four candles: one blue, one red, one yellow, and one brown or green. Put these at the western, southern, eastern, and northern points of your work room, respectively. Also have long-handled matches ready, and if you wish one white candle (or one that you've made) in the center of the space to represent Spirit.
2. Settle into the central part of your work space. Breathe deeply and center your spirit, focusing your mind on your goals for this day.
3. Light one of the matches and walk to the eastern candle. Put the flame to the wick saying:

Guardians and Watchtowers of the east, I call and charge you.
Come, protect this sacred space and breathe on me with the winds of
inspiration and learning.

4. Move clockwise to the southern candle. As you go, visualize a line of white light connecting the two points together. Put the flame to the wick saying:

Guardians and Watchtowers of the south, I call and charge you.
Come protect this sacred space and ignite in me the spark of magic.

   Note that you may need to keep your hand in front of the match head so the flame doesn't go out while you're moving.

5. Continue moving clockwise to the western candle. Visualize the line of energy/power connected to both the southern and the eastern candle by radiant light. Put the flame to the wick saying:

Guardians and Watchtowers of the west, I call and charge you.
Come protect this sacred space and wash over me with waves of
insight and discernment.

6. Continue on to the northern candle extending your visualization, and putting the flame to the wick (or if necessary, lighting a fresh match first) saying:

Guardians and Watchtowers of the north, I call and charge you.
Come protect this sacred space and grant me strong foundations
from which to grow.

7. Finally move back to the center saying:

Great Spirit, Guides, and Ancient Ones, I welcome you to this time
of creation and study. Help me in my tasks this day—fill the pages
of my Book of Shadows with your wisdom and blessing. So be it.

   Light the central candle (if you've used one) and visualize the outlines of your circle now slowly expanding to create a complete sphere of protection all around, above, and below you. Begin working on your book.

When you're done working on the book for the day, you should thank the powers who have protected and guided you in some manner, and then bid them farewell. You can do this through a brief prayer like:

God/dess, Guides, Ancestors, Powers of Creation—thank you for joining me here today and blessing the work of my hands. As you leave this place, carry the positive energy created to any in need. Walk with me daily that I might follow the Path of Beauty in confidence and peace. Farewell.

A prayer like this one accomplishes much. It gives thanks for what you've been given, and a thankful heart is one ready to both give and receive. It seeks to bless others, and by so doing you, too, will receive blessings. Finally, it acknowledges that magical living isn't limited to a few hours here and there, but is part of every moment of every day.

Blessing and Energizing Your Book

I said earlier that your Book of Shadows is really never done because humans never stop growing and changing until we leave our bodies. Even so, at some points during your spiritual sojourn you'll find your spellbook seems quite complete. At these junctures it's good to pause for a moment and bless this wonderful magical tool.

Blessing augments the energy you've created thus far within the pages of your tome. It eliminates any stray negatives that might have entered in from simple human error, and supports the positives so that they shine like jewels. In other words, blessing your Book of Shadows is similar to putting icing on the cake—it makes everything a little nicer and a little more complete. A blessing binds all the elements of your Book of Shadows into a harmonious whole.

Exactly what form your blessing takes will vary according to the magical tradition you've chosen to follow. Most blessings, however, use the human hand as a focal point through which divine energy flows. One blessing I personally like is an adaptation of an old Gaelic prayer. You might like it too, so consider adding it into your spellbook under "Meditations, Visualizations, and Prayers." It goes like this:

> *God and Goddess guide me; God and Goddess sustain me*
> *God and Goddess stand before me as an example*
> *God and Goddess watch behind me to protect*
> *God and Goddess live within me and the pages of this book*
> *let it inspire and direct my journey*
> *as I walk on your path; and you abide in my steps.*

As it is written, so let it be done.

PART II

Spellbook Structure

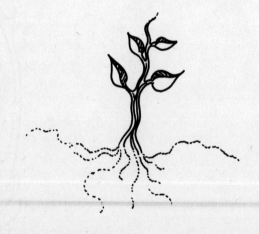

*T*here could potentially be as many ways of putting together a good Book of Shadows as there are people in the world. After all, each of us has our own inner vision of the Divine, and a slightly different way of understanding, integrating, and working magic. This situation left with me with a very difficult question. How could I design a spellbook formula that would suit everyone who reads this book?

Well, the truth is that I couldn't. All I can do is give you some ideas, hints, and guidance derived from my fourteen years of study, research, and hands-on magical practice. I decided to include thirteen possible sections to use for creating and organizing your core Book of Shadows. Thirteen represents the number of moon cycles in a year and the number of people in a traditional coven, so it has the right type of energy for patterning the spellbook's outline.

These are the sections I've selected:

- Magical symbols and tools
- Prayer, meditation, and visualization
- Sacred Space: creating and maintaining
- Spells and spell components
- Charms, amulets, talismans, and fetishes
- The Wheel of Life (personal and seasonal rituals and timing)
- Divination tools and methods
- Elements, correspondences, and applications
- Food and beverage correspondences and applications
- Color, sound, texture, aromatic, and number correspondences
- Crystals, metals, mineral, and fossil correspondences
- Plant and animal correspondences and applications
- Gods and Goddess correspondences (powers, attributes, culture, etc.)

You can use these divisions as they stand or come up with a completely different tact, but decide from the get-go how you want the book organized when it's done. Otherwise you're liable to go to considerable time and expense in reinventing the wheel! Bear in mind throughout your decision-making process that your completed Book of Shadows is something that should:

- Act as an effective resource and reference tool for any magical theories, correspondences, and methods that you use regularly.
- Include ideas that you want to mull over and tinker with.
- Inspire you to walk the Path of Beauty with strength, love, courage, peace, and truthfulness.
- Include step-by-step instructions for all preferred techniques; even when you master these, you'll probably want to share the information with novices later.
- Include progressive methodology that meets the needs of changing times.
- Motivate personal growth (e.g. include some really challenging things that will take time to master).
- Create a portrait of modern magic as it applies directly to your life and vision.

Once you know how you ultimately want your spellbook assembled and have everything in place to start writing or typing the pages of the text, you're ready to begin. Start going through the sections of this book and transferring the ideas and information that you find most useful into the appropriate parts of your own Book of Shadows. Add in other information you've gathered on your own along with personal insights, leaving plenty of room for more additions later.

There are some simple steps you can take to ensure that the outcome of this process is as positive and fulfilling as possible:

1. Tackle only one portion of information at a time. Read it over, meditate about it, and pray for guidance. This gives you an important opportunity to really think about that one facet of your magical life and practice, and its meaning to you.

2. Don't rush step one. Take as much time as you need with each section's material and insights. For one thing, if you try to learn and assimilate too much too quickly, you'll reach mental overload. For another thing, you have a lifetime to create a formalized Book of Shadows. Rushing often precedes mistakes or sloppiness that you're bound to regret in retrospect.

3. Since human needs rarely evidence themselves at convenient times, you can refer to other sections of this book before you've studied them to answer questions or get specific instructions. Just don't let this "sneak preview" distract you from returning to the original studies unless Spirit really leads you to continue in that section.

4. If you read anything here, or in any other book, that makes you uncomfortable or goes against personal taboos, *do not use* that procedure, method, tool, component, or whatever. In magic, it is extremely important that you listen to your gut instincts and the voice of Spirit in your heart. You are your own guru, your own High Priest or Priestess—no book can take that place in your life.

5. Personalize, practice, and be patient. Personalization keeps everything meaningful and vibrant, practice leads to magical adeptness, and patience makes the entire learning process a little easier to bear. We live in an "instant" society, and spiritual progress is not instantaneous. Remind yourself of this, keeping hope in your heart, your eyes on the horizon, and your feet firmly on the path.

How to Use This Book

In looking at the remainder of this book, the process of assembling your own spellbook might seem overwhelming at first. There's research to be done, notes to make, organizing to complete, and even a bit of cross-referencing to consider. Before this puts you off, take a deep breath and remember that Rome wasn't built in a day—your Book of Shadows certainly won't be constructed quickly either. For some people this is a lifelong process, but I'm willing to guess that it will take you at the minimum several months to complete your work and create a fulfilling, functional spellbook.

To help out a bit, I suggest you read through this book from cover to cover before starting anything. As you do, make an outline for yourself (similar to the one at the opening of this section) that lists different spellbook topics and where you eventually want them to go in your finished Book of Shadows. For example, say you want to have a part that covers gods and goddesses, how to honor them, associations and powers, and the like. You would then scan through this text and write down all the pages on which related entries occur, and include the brief notes that explain the importance of the entry. Then go through other related books and do likewise (be sure to note each page, paragraph, etc. on which significant information appears). Afterward, you can reorder these notes in any manner that fits your vision and creative eye!

Why bother to go to such lengths? The reason is actually three-fold. First, this isn't just any book—it's going to be your bible (of sorts). What you put in the final work is going to matter a lot, to you as a person and as a spiritual being. Taking a little extra time to sort, consider, compile, and finally refine the material will result in your Book of Shadows becoming part of you on an intimate, internalized level, not just on paper.

Second, throughout this text I've given you ideas on where to cross-reference or copy information into other sections of your spellbook. This cross-referencing or repetition is important because everything in magic is interrelated. Metaphysical techniques, mediums, and ideas create a tightly woven web where it's nearly impossible to talk about one type of magic of method without touching on another. You'll quickly start to see what I mean as you read. Consequently, as you assemble your spellbook, you'll want everything necessary for understanding and utilizing the core subjects in *one spot* (unless you like thumbing through dozens of pages to find things). Alternatively, you'll need to create an ongoing index for your Book of Shadows so that it won't take hours to get the information you need, when you need it.

Third, and perhaps most important, by the time you're done with the process I'm suggesting, you'll be pretty darn close to having exactly what you want for the "good copy" of that particular section in your spellbook. Think of each step along the way as analogous to an artist creating a fine masterpiece. He or she studies their subject in depth first—they get to know it from many different angles. Next comes rough outlines, shading, detailed lines, and then finally finishing touches that slowly, perceptibly bring the work to life. Your Book of Shadows will have such a life and soul when you're done. It is, after all, the art of your heart and spirit.

1

Magical Symbols and Tools

In magic, you'll quickly discover that tools and symbols are nearly inseparable from one another, which is why I've included them together as a section for your Book of Shadows. As you read this section, it's important to remember that a symbol is no less potent than what it represents in the sacred space. For example, since a cup has basically a circular shape, it can "become" the goddess, the element of water, or the moon in the sacred space (the womb of creation)! Anything bearing a lozenge or oval shape can be used similarly. This means that symbols, tools, and their respective meanings give us a lot of material to work with in designing a truly personalized, visionary religious system.

Magical Symbols

Truthfully, nearly any shape or design can become a magical symbol simply by intending it to be so, then using it accordingly. However, having something to start with helps! Throughout human history people have used basic geometric shapes to represent what they perceived as important archetypes in the universe. Exactly what each shape meant in each setting varied, of course, since symbolism is highly subjective. Be that as it may, symbols are very important to all magical work. We use them in visualization, we use them in spells, we even use them in the way we move in the sacred circle.

So, how does one choose which symbols to include in a Book of Shadows? That's not an easy question, but any symbols that strike a strong immediate response deep within you are worth consideration. Also symbols that you connect quickly with a specific meaning are good choices for inclusion. For example, if you asked most people what a red cross represents, they'd likely say something like "health" or "blood" without too much thought. These are the kinds of symbols you're looking for—those that you instinctively *know* and associate with a one- or two-word theme.

For the purpose of this study, I've confined the following list to common, easily drawn emblems. Some more complex or culturally-specific designs will come up in different sections of this book (like runes in the divination section). You can cross-reference these designs to this part of your spellbook, or copy them into it as desired.

Ankh

While more useful to those practicing an Egyptian form of magic, the symbol of the ankh has been adopted by popular culture and is a wonderful representation of life's vital energy and fertility. *Hint:* For those who follow either Osiris or Isis as deities, the ankh is a suitable holy symbol for you to use in honoring these powers. Transfer this information into the gods/goddess section of your spellbook.

Cauldron (See also Tools)

The cauldron has some associations with the triangle because of its three legs, yet its shape makes it a symbol of the goddess, especially in her generative aspect. In many religious myths, when someone drinks from the goddess's well, they receive inspiration, visions, magical knowledge, healing, or become immortal. In Wicca, a cauldron is often part of ritual work, and some people like to keep one on their altar to represent the feminine force of creation. *Special note for your god and goddess section:* The cauldron can represent Indra (India), Odin (Norse), Cerridwen (Celtic), the Lady of the Lake (Arthurian), the Fates (Greco-Roman), and Wyrd (Saxon) just to name a few!

Circle

One of the most important symbols for Wicca, the circle represents oneness and the ever-moving wheel of time and life. Wiccans meet in circles, a protected sacred space, to show that each member is an important part of the whole, and a part of the magic ultimately created.

Historically speaking, circles have been used as a base symbol to help represent many other things. For example, a circle with a dot in the middle equates to the sun, three interlocking circles represent the trinities of body-mind-spirit, son-father-grandfather, and maiden-mother-crone.

Cross

Many cultures used a cross to represent the meeting point around which the four seasons, directions, elements, etc. revolved. Crossroads, in numerous settings, similarly symbolize a meeting ground between this world and the next. Among the Celts, crosses were always equidistant to visually depict balance between the mental and spiritual, masculine and feminine, sounds and silences.

Interestingly, crosses are symbols of more than just the Christian savior. Wotan had a cross, as did Frey, Asshur (Assyrian), Anu (Assyrian), Indra (India), and Hecate (Greek), just to name a few. *Hint:* Copy this last paragraph into your section on gods and goddesses or cross-reference it for future use.

Dot or Point

The dot or point symbolizes the self and a place of beginnings. It represents creativity, making something out of nothing, and focus on and attention to detail. It denotes an end and a new start or emphasis, as in a period at the end of a sentence. *Hint:* Use a dot as a focal point for meditation to fix your attention, then slowly let your vision blur. Make notes of this technique and its success or failure in your meditation section of the spellbook.

Hexagram

In Judaic tradition, this is the Star of David and Seal of Solomon, both of which have protective, fortune-bringing power. If you think of the hexagram as two interconnected triangles (one pointing up, and the other pointing down) you can see why this association exists. These two triangles bring balance and unity between male and female, the elements, and humankind and divinity. Hexagrams appear frequently in old grimoires as part of spirit-calling rituals, or potent spells where extra precaution was prudent.

Knot

Knots represent the sometimes tangled course of destiny, and they're also a very potent symbol of binding or releasing energy. For example, in many marriage rituals the woman's knots (hair or clothing) would be untied to encourage fertility. In some modern magical traditions, the number of knots in one's belt represents a specific level of magical achievement.

In Russian and Hebrew mystical traditions magic was so strongly tied with this symbol that the word for Witch or Wizard translates as "knot tier." In several other settings the word knot is synonymous with amulet! This makes the knot an excellent symbol to use for containing or liberating any energy we create. *Hint:* You may want to copy this last information into your spell section, or cross-reference it there.

Line

A line marks one's boundaries or territory. It carves out a path, or creates a division over which you will not pass. It denotes finding direction. A line moving upward has more spiritual connotations, while one moving left to right deals with Earthly matters. An angled line to the right might represent keeping one foot on the ground, while one angled slightly to the left might symbolize striving for spiritual "uprightness."

Pentagram

Basically the Witch's cross, the pentagram represents all the elements working together with the self and spirit to create magic. In many ancient settings the pentagram depicted authority, protection, and truthfulness. Modern Wiccans often correlate each point with something specific, the top being Spirit or Ether. Moving clockwise from this point, the right top point is the element of Air and the seat of human intellect, the right bottom point is the Earth and material concerns, the left bottom point is Fire and passion, and the left top point is Water and the seat of our emotions. (Mind you, this varies depending on who you talk to.)

Spiral

Ancient people in many cultures used the spiral as a symbol of growth or diminishing (depending on its direction), natural and human cycles, and the ebb and flow of time itself. When moving inward, the spiral can symbolize self-focus, the will, or deep meditative states. A spiral moving outward manifests that will and whatever was learned from Spirit in moments of quiet reflection. Finally, twin, or double, spirals represent opposites—the yin/yang—melding into a harmonious oneness as in DNA. *Hint:* Visualize a inward moving spiral around the area of your navel when you need to center and ground yourself. Copy this technique into the visualization section of your spellbook, along with the results achieved.

Square

The square represents the four corners of creation, the elements (Earth-Air-Fire-Water), the four seasons, the four-part day (sunrise, noon, sunset, midnight), equinoxes and solstices (as well as cross-quarter days), stability, truthfulness, and safety. The square provides foundations to our dreams. It is the "real" world within which we make concrete efforts to help manifest our magic.

> *Think about it:* A square is very important to creating sacred space because we use the four points (Earth/north, Air/east, Fire/south, Water/west) as the "dots" around which the sphere of protection is cast. This provides safety and foundations for your magic!

Star

In humankind's ancient past the stars were alive and, as any spirit, participated in human affairs. Some gods and goddesses resided in the stars, while other goddesses had stars as sacred symbols or as part of their name including Astarte, Venus, and Diana. In modern times, stars are most strongly connected to wish magic, goal-oriented spells, and to the prophetic art of astrology, which will be briefly covered under divination.

Thor's Hammer

Similar in construction to a Tao cross (which looks like a T), Thor's hammer is most suited to those called to a Norse tradition, but has been popularized in recent years through jewelry. What most people don't know is that this symbol has been a favorite protective amulet for thousands of years! And, Thor is not the only one to bear a potent hammer either—Ananke, a Greek goddess of fortune, used a hammer to create human destinies and literally linked our souls forever with the ancient powers!

Triangle

A triangle represents both the triune nature (see circles) and a kind of stability between the energies that war within us. The mind wants us to think, the body wants us to feel, and the spirit wants us to *be*. Since the perfect triangle has equal sides, this is also what we strive for: balance.

The triangle is the base symbol for the pyramids, one of the greatest representations of human spirit seeking after the divine. A downward pointing triangle is a feminine symbol; the upward pointing triangle is considered masculine.

Wheel

In Wicca, all things are part of a great wheel, which implies continual motion and progress. The sun rises, sets, and returns again. People are born, live, and are then reborn to a new existence. This is one reason why the annual cycle of Wicca is represented by an eight-pointed wheel—the center of which is the individual. Also, there is an excellent example of wheel symbolism and interpretive values in all Tarot decks: The Wheel of Fortune (see divination section for more insights). Wheels are another popular emblem for various deities including Arianrhod (Celtic) Kali (India), Vortumna (Etruscan), and Fortuna (Rome).

Here is a list of some other symbols that you may wish to research for inclusion in your Book of Shadows:

signs of the zodiac	horseshoe	arrow
labyrinth-maze	scale	trident
body parts-positions	mirror	thread
planetary symbols	web	key

Once you've compiled such a list, the next obvious question becomes, what do you do with it? You can do a lot of things. Say, for example, you're trying to come up with a good spell or charm to help safeguard a relationship that's on the rocks. Reading over your list of symbols, you notice a heart for love, and the circle for protection. From here putting together a spell or charm becomes much simpler. For example, take the image of a heart and draw a circle around it in salt on your altar. Leave this in place until the negativity passes

In much the same manner symbols can be added into visualization, path working, and ritual. The only real rule is that all the symbols used must represent the goal at hand, and must also work harmoniously together.

Magical Tools and Uses

The more you practice magic, the more you will come to realize that tools aren't necessary to our art, but they are helpful. Each implement directs our internal and external attention to something specific, to an energy imprint lodged deep within our being. Using tools correctly, therefore, can help us release latent magical and psychic skills or apply them more effectively.

The best way to understand this is to think about putting a nail into the floor. You could try to do this with your hand, or perhaps a rock, but a hammer will certainly make the job easier. That's what magical implements do for the practitioner—they add extra sensual dimensions and become helpmates for moving and directing energy.

In terms of deciding what tools to put into this particular collection, I felt it most important to cover those that appear frequently in rituals and spellcraft no matter the magical path. From this list you can pick out those you work with (or want to work with) the most and copy the information into your spellbook along with any other bits of history, folklore, and personal insights you may have.

Note that more culturally or situationally specific tools will come up periodically throughout this book, like poppets for spell work. Consider cross-referencing these sections in your own Book of Shadows.

Athame

Traditionally an athame is a two-edged ritual knife that represents the two-edged nature of magic and the opposites of all creation. Magical energy, in and of itself, is neutral. Only when we put that energy into motion does it take on polarity and purpose. This is one reason why White Witches use the motto "harm none." This phrase, along with the athame, gently reminds us that magic can hurt as well as heal if we're not careful.

Some wiccans use their ritual knife for harvesting magical herbs, while others keep it set aside for use only in the sacred space to represent the god, scribe the circle, direct magical energy like a pointer, and to open astral doorways when necessary. The first application is more folksy, taking the attitude "if it's handy, use it!" The second application is found more often in High or ritualistic magic.

In symbolic recreations of the Great Rite, the athame embodies the force of the masculine energies of the universe. It is then united with the feminine powers: the cup. Note that some witches prefer a wand or even the pointer finger of their strong hand as an alternative to the athame.

Brazier

The brazier rightfully represents the Fire element in the context of the sacred circle (really, any fire-safe container will do for this purpose). The use of a brazier goes back to the days when tribes gathered around a central fire for all important community celebrations and observances. In this case, your tribe is the people with whom you practice, if any. The brazier also represents the warmth and kinship of the hearth fire, around which your magical family gathers to celebrate its ties and unity.

Note that when rituals are held outdoors, the brazier can be replaced with a cauldron filled with burning embers, torches, or a well-tended fire pit. When you burn a symbol of your wish in a ritual fire, especially during Beltane, it should come to pass within a year and a day if it's meant to be. Additionally, ritual fires are an excellent place to burn away unwanted characteristics, bad luck, or negativity. (*These two last points are good entries for your spell section.*)

Candles

Lighting a candle can represent the presence of Spirit in a sacred circle, or it can be a way of honoring the Watchtowers. Blowing out a candle represents completion, subdual, and dispersing power. Candles are the favored tool for Candlemas (Imbolc) and during the solstice as a way of honoring the sun's return. *Note:* You may want to include this idea in your section on the "Wheel of Life" under "seasonal rituals."

Beyond this, Wiccans often use candles as focal points for meditation, divination, and spellcraft because the color, scent, and fire all combine for very flexible symbolism. For example, jumping over a candle can represent fertility or a new beginning; or, burning a green candle with a dollar sign in it is a way of encouraging prosperity. *Hint:* Transfer these last two ideas into the spells section of your Book of Shadows if you like them.

Cauldron

In a ritual context, the cauldron's three legs represent the three-fold nature of both the divine and humankind. Therefore, what the cauldron holds is of particular significance to the rite. During spring the cauldron might hold rich soil to symbolize fertile beginnings or water since spring is a rainy season. Come summer the cauldron might hold kindling, in fall it can hold a bounty of harvested foods, and in winter it might be filled with ice, then melted to encourage the sun's return! Note, however, that the way each person, or each group, uses the cauldron changes depending on the celebration and tradition involved.

Note that the surface of a cauldron (or a cup), when filled with water, can be used as a scrying device. More about this type of divination will be covered in the section of the book on divination tools-methods.

Chalice, Cup, or Bowl

This round, womblike object is the partner to the athame, being symbolic of the Goddess, Water, and the Moon. People often share a cup during group rituals as a sign of unity. (This tradition is also part of pagan marriage rites). *Hint:* With this in mind, you might want to add cups to your spellcraft section as a potential component for love-related magic (perhaps filled with a love potion!). For a really good study on the cup and its meaning, look through the cups suit of the Tarot and meditate on each card separately.

Herbs, Flowers, and Other Aromatics

Wiccans often strew the edge of a sacred space with symbolic flowers or herbs to strengthen the protective energy or stress the theme of the gathering. Burning herbs, flowers, or incense has similar effect, except that the smoke also clears away negative energies and represents our prayers reaching ever upward. The choice of aromatic is dependent on the spell, meditation, or ritual. More insights on the effective use of aromatics will be given in several other parts of this book including: food and beverage correspondences, spells, and plant and animal correspondences.

God or Goddess Image

This isn't necessary, but a lot of people like to have statuary or other items that represent the divine. Any god can be symbolized by a long object like a crystal wand (i.e., a phallic symbol). Any goddess can be represented by round items like a tumbled crystal (i.e., a womblike symbol). But, if you're following a specific god or goddess, you should try to find out what objects or symbols were sacred to him or her, then use something along those lines in your ritual space to honor that presence.

Robes and Masks

You know the old saying "clothes make a person." Well that's the whole idea behind using robes and masks in ritual. It helps us separate ourselves from the workaday world and connect more intimately with a specific type of energy or spirit. For example, someone practicing a neoshamanic magical tradition might use animal masks to help him understand and commune with his totem and animal helpers in the astral world.

In a ritual wherein a specific god or goddess is called into the sacred space, the priest or priestess can wear a mask representing that power. In this case, however, the mask helps the priest or priestess literally accept the role of that presence and become a channel for divine energy. For the participants watching, the mask signals the change occurring and helps them focus on the shifting energies rather than one individual.

Robes work similarly, except they distribute the vibrations that you carry throughout your aura more evenly (instead of focusing on the face). They flow, like we wish our magic to flow. I should note too that the use of the word robe here is somewhat subjective. For some people a T-tunic and belt becomes a robe and for others an elaborate Celtic dress becomes a robe. Just like in a theatrical play, the character's costume suits that individual and setting.

Sword

Swords are an alternative to the athame. Because of the size difference, some practitioners like to use these to invoke the quarters using the tip to scribe symbols in the air or to open and close formal doorways into and out of the circle once sacred space is created. To jump over a sword in a wedding ritual marks the end of single life and encourages fertility. A good study of the extent of a sword's symbolism may be found in the sword suit of the Tarot.

Wand

Yet again, the wand can substitute for an athame, especially in a setting where edged weapons aren't acceptable. The wand has a softer energy signature, however, since it has no cutting edges. It represents authority, a way to direct energy (like a pointer), and, thanks to the fairy godmother, it also symbolizes positive change.

Note that some individuals use a large walking staff in a manner similar to a wand. Both items often bear decorations like carvings and inlaid compatible crystals to further augment the energy they create. Wands equate to rods in the Tarot.

Modern Alternatives

The neat thing about living in today's world is that technology gives us a lot of fun alternatives to traditional tools, so please don't limit yourself to the list here. Sometimes I like to use a wooden spoon as a wand to cast the circle for food magic, for example. A kitchen sink can similarly become a very large "cup," your stove a symbol of the Fire element or a substitute for a candle, and the like. *Hint:* Transfer these ideas to your food and beverage section.

So, look around your living space, and in fact the whole world, with a creative eye. Everything has potential for magic—it's all in your perspective. More information like this will also be covered in the section on spell components.

Care and Keeping

Once you have your magical tools assembled, it's important to take proper care of them. Claim them before the powers of Creation as your own. Bless and empower them for the tasks for which you plan to use them.

Also find a way to store them safely (both physically and psychically) between uses. For example, get a small storage box, sprinkle it with some cedar or sandalwood, and cover this with white cloth for purity and cleansing. Tuck all your goods neatly inside!

If you have an altar that's out of reach of pets and children, many tools can remain there, ready for use as you have need. Mind you, if these start gathering dust always clean them off before beginning any magical procedure to eliminate any lingering energy that could muck things up. What's most important is that you always treat your chosen tools with the appropriate respect and acknowledge their part in making your daily magical tradition deeply meaningful and personal.

Personal Notes

2

Prayer, Meditation, and Visualization

Like tools and symbols, prayer, meditation, and visualization are strongly linked to one another. In fact, prayer frequently precedes meditation, while meditation often includes visualization! So, we'll cover all three dimensions in this section of your Book of Shadows.

So, what about these three techniques do you want to include in your spellbook? For starters, I suggest combining step-by-step instructional material with some specific examples and good definitions. The definitions will help you understand the goal of each exercise. Examples help you internalize that understanding and put the knowledge to work in your spiritual life. The step-by-step instructions act like training wheels for your first attempts so you know where to go and how to get there safely.

In each of the three subsections that follow, I'll be going over this kind of information. Use what works for you, and tweak the rest. As you go through these subsections, don't forget to add any special prayers, meditations, or visualizations that you've already found particularly successful or fulfilling. Reminder: Always note your sources!

Prayer

Some Wiccans find the idea of praying uncomfortable because it reminds them too much of mainstream churches. Other people feel awkward about communicating with higher powers, as if that's a role best suited to a priest or priestess. If you find yourself in either group, relax. There's nothing "churchy" about magical prayers, and one part of the process of writing your Book of Shadows is accepting your role as your own guru, priest, or priestess.

Think of prayer as nothing more than talking sincerely to your image of the divine, and I think you'll find the whole process more "user friendly." Prayers don't have to be fancy, there need be no King James–styled flowery phrases, and you don't even have to pray out loud. Our thoughts are prayers uttered inwardly. What's most important about our prayers is candor—you can't hide who or what you are, in the depths of your soul, from the Ancient Powers, so be yourself.

Prayer Phraseology

Most prayers begin with some kind of acknowledgment of the power that one is hoping to contact. That power might be a generic "god," "goddess," "great spirit," "ancient one," or "all." These designations are a good choice if you haven't chosen a specific god or goddess to follow, or if you're not really sure of exactly how this immense power should be envisioned or addressed.

Next comes the body of the prayer (or your heart-to-heart talk with the god/dess). During this conversation, we might ask for something, say thank you for manifested magic, and honor the divine powers by our words and respectfulness. No matter the content, however, the result is usually the same: an improvement in attitude, a sense of peace, and renewed hope.

The windup of Wiccan prayers often includes the maxim "for the greatest good, and it harm none." This is also true of spells. This particular expression represents a core philosophy in all positive magic. It is also a phrase that I highly recommend you put in

---

PRAYER ASSEMBLY

1. Opening supplication to, and greeting of, the sacred powers, either by name or by some generic designation

2. Purpose of the prayer: sharing your needs, honoring the divine presence that has helped meet those goals, and an indication of thankfulness

3. Closing: a set of words that concludes your devotional time and neatly wraps up the energy created

---

the front of your Book of Shadows as an ongoing reminder that we should never seek to harm or manipulate with our power. By adding this maxim to the end of our prayer, we allow the sacred powers to step in and respond to our prayers-spells with the best possible answer, even if it wasn't exactly what we wanted or expected. Remember, *"for the greatest good"* doesn't automatically mean what you *think* is good.

Another concluding phrase used in magical prayers is *"so mote it be"* or *"so be it."* This equates to the Wiccan version of "amen." It provides closure to both the prayer and the energy it created.

Finally, you will regularly hear a Wiccan benediction at the end of a gathering's prayers. It goes: "Merry meet, merry part, and merry meet again!" This is a blessing that says we meet freely in an atmosphere of joy and mutual respect, we leave freely carrying happiness and magic with us, and when we come together again it will be with joyful hearts.

Here is one example of a prayer that you might want to add to your Book of Shadows. It comes from my own:

> *Great Spirit, show me the way*
> *to walk with the light, to dance the stones*
> *to receive visions at night, and know I'm never alone*
> *to reach for the stars, with a wish in one hand*
> *to reach for the Earth, and help heal our land*

to follow my bliss, to live happy and free,
Great Spirit show me that the magic is me
So mote it be.

You'll notice that I used rhyme here, but that's not necessary for your own prayers. I just find it a handy mnemonic device that frees my mind to focus wholly on the intention behind what I'm saying. Also, prayers do not need to be precontrived. Whenever you feel the need to talk to the Powers, do so! The more you stay in communion with the Sacred, the more it becomes part of your daily reality.

Meditation

As you create this section in your Book of Shadows, you'll want to have one part that describes the various meditation techniques you know, and another part that gives meditations that are aimed at specific goals. Additionally, you may want to include path working here. This is a type of very detailed meditation that requires making choices and becoming interactive with the exercise.

In terms of techniques for meditation, I think you'll find the following information useful for starters:

1. Most meditations boil down to contemplating one subject or situation very seriously, privately, and from as many different angles as possible.
2. Successful meditation usually requires a quiet place void of normal interruptions, so turn off your phone and ask housemates to honor your privacy for a set period of time.
3. Learn slow, rhythmic breathing techniques. For centering yourself, I suggest inhaling deeply through your nose and exhaling slowly by mouth. Keep repeating this pattern until one breath moves effortlessly into the next and the cares of day fade away. *Note:* Nearly *all* esoteric traditions use breathing as an integral part of achieving deep meditative states.
4. If you find you're having trouble concentrating when you meditate, try listening to the sound of your breath as it mingles with

your heartbeat. These two rhythms have a natural ability to generate a semi-meditative state.

5. Another way to guide your mind away from temporal matters is through the use of sound. One of the most ancient mantras, the *Om* of Hindu origins, is very popular in Wicca too. Why? Because the sound represents the universe and self in harmony. It is the "I am" that affirms existence and turns our thoughts inward to view and contemplate spiritual matters.

There are all kinds of sounds you can use while meditating from simple vowels to full magical chants. Both types of verbalizations fill the air around you and your auric field with positive energy that accents your goal. Just make sure you choose the sounds-words so that they're in keeping with the focus of your meditation. If you can't speak openly due to external circumstances, verbalize the sound in your mind. This will fill your mind and body with the same energies as a spoken phrase would.

Next, the goals of each meditation will obviously vary depending on personal need and desire. However, in reviewing esoteric traditions around the world there seem to be some core themes under which nearly every meditation can be categorized. These themes are:

RELAXATION   Be it for health purposes or simply to calm one's soul after a busy day, the process of meditation has a natural restful side effect. Considering the pace of today's society, this may be the most important gift meditation offers us, a chance to still our spirits and simply listen to the Universe. *Hint:* Relaxation meditations require little in the way of personal preparation. You can sit or lie down, quiet your mind, and simply breathe. As your tensions wane, more oxygen gets into every part of your body, improving the healthful, peaceful qualities of your meditation.

COMPREHENSION   Meditation helps us integrate what we've learned or experienced so that eventually we can begin manifesting it outwardly as part of our every day life. This type of meditation doesn't require visualization, but the overall success can be increased by adding visualization into the process. For example, when you're mulling over the meaning of a dream, visualizing that dream again often makes it clearer and helps you recall more details. *Hint:* Transfer this information on comprehension into the dream section of your personal magical diary (covered in Part III).

PREPARATION   In a more religious environment, meditation is one way of readying one's spirit for communing with the divine or other entities, like guides, devas, and the Ancestors.

Point to Ponder: Wicca can be a philosophy or a religious system. Which is it for you? Make notes of your feelings in the insight-introspection part of your magical diary.

Note that this kind of preparation is necessary to many mystical procedures to ready one's body, mind, and spirit to receive and effectively use specific kinds of energy, as occurs with healing and channeling.

SEPARATION   In certain metaphysical processes, like divination or mediumship, meditation helps detach us from ourselves and personal opinions to see the bigger picture. The idea here is to figuratively "let go and let god" so that the readings provided are filled with Spirit instead of self and ego. *Hint:* Transfer this last information into the divination section of your spellbook, or cross-reference it there.

Beyond this, separation improves personal perspective. When you can't see the proverbial forest for the trees, step back and look through the eyes of Spirit. This particular theme merges slightly with the next one, clarification.

CLARIFICATION   When we find a particularly enigmatic issue (spiritual or mundane), meditation gives us a medium through which we can look at it differently, as a casual observer rather than a participant. This clarification process requires the addition of visualization. Meditating using visualization is like watching a movie during which you can take mental notes of things that you didn't consciously observe before. Then, bring whatever you learn in the meditation back and apply it to the matter at hand. *Important:* All metaphysical techniques require that we remain active participants in our well-being and future. Sacred powers and spiritual insights will help us, if we are willing to likewise help ourselves.

Seven Meditation Helps and Hints

I know that I sometimes have trouble meditating. When you experience the figurative brick wall with personal meditations, here are some hints to keep in your Book of Shadows and refer back to for help:

1. Add aromatics. Dab on some essential oil (sandalwood is ideal), burn incense, or whatever. Key the chosen aroma to the goal of the meditation. Refer to the list of plant correspondences or spell components for ideas.
2. Darken the room. Bright light speaks to the conscious, logical self. Darkness or candle light helps release the intuitive, lunar nature.
3. Add quiet background music. This shouldn't be something that distracts you, but rather let it add another sensual cue to the equation. I find that instrumental music works best.
4. Practice, practice, practice. Since meditation is a discipline, most people won't get adept at it overnight. Our minds are used to thinking about many things at once; now you're asking it to focus on one subject and only that subject, so be patient with yourself and keep trying. Eventually you'll breach the barriers of an itchy foot and uncomfortable arms and simply find yourself where you need to be mentally.
5. Try each meditation more than once. The second time might prove more successful just from familiarity. Also, when using

meditation for clarity and comprehension, each repetition reveals new insights!

6. Make notes of your successes and failures, then try to figure out what defined each. For example, a simple interruption could cause the failure of a meditation one day, but in solitude the same meditation proves totally successful the next time. The ingredients that create a successful meditation once will likely do so again.

7. Transfer your most successful meditations into your Book of Shadows so you can use them again as needed, or adapt them to other circumstances.

> *Note:* All of these extra dimensions help with spellcraft, divination, rituals, etc. They are effective aids to nearly any metaphysical procedure you undertake.

Visualization

Do you remember daydreaming when you were younger? You know, those visions of the "happily ever after" life, secret places you retreated to in your mind, and fantasies of magical realms? This kind of daydream is exactly what visualization advocates. The only difference is that instead of randomly letting your mind wander, you will now be directing its attention and creating the imagery.

To marry a visualization with a meditation isn't difficult, it just takes a little forethought. Here are a few guidelines that I use to design visualizations. If you find them helpful, add them to this section of your spellbook:

1. Think about which symbol or image best represents your goal.
2. In considering symbolism, stick with what you know. While multiculturalism has its time and place, symbols and imagery from societies other than that with which you're familiar probably won't be very helpful. You need to have a strong

mental and emotional understanding of the pictures-symbols in your visualization for them to effectively translate into energy patterns.

3. Make the symbol or image you've chosen the nucleus around which your entire visualization revolves. For example, if you've chosen a tree as the focal point, make sure you start and end the visualization at that tree.

4. Have the visualization follow a sequence of events that make sense and result in the positive manifestation of the goal (literally or symbolically). For example, when you go back to the tree in number 3, if you've used this as a representation of building personal strength, see yourself as part of the tree, growing strong and sure with deep, solid roots.

5. Give yourself time after the visualization to think about anything unexpected that you experienced, and also whether or not the visualization was successful. Make notes of your immediate impressions so you can return to them later for more insight. *Note:* You probably want to keep these notes in the personal diary portion of your spellbook, or in a separate scrap paper file. That way you can pull out the real gems and leave the random ramblings aside.

In my travels I've noticed that an awful lot of people have trouble visualizing things, and ask for advice on combating this problem. Part of the problem seems to come from a society that provides us with external stimulus constantly (notably on television). Those of us who grew up sitting in front of the television set always had images fed to us instead of having to create them in our minds. So, we need to learn to imagine again.

Since this seems to be such a common problem, I recommend putting these hints in your Book of Shadows for those times when you find activating your imagination is kind of difficult:

1. Remember that a visualization doesn't have to be complex to be effective. So, start simply. Close your eyes and see a line or a circle (geometrics seem easiest for most people).

Note: Get out of the "fancier is better" pattern of thinking here and now. In magic, both the simple and the sublime have value and both options should be considered.

2. From here, slowly add other lines or shapes until you've built the symbol or image you wanted. Returning to the tree again, from an artist's perspective a tree shape is basically made of a circle at the top and a rectangle at the bottom. Create these outlines in your mind's eye, then color them in with shades and texture, using the crayons of your imagination.
3. Don't feel silly. There is nothing foolish about wanting to be able to see things in a different way. It's what shamans, psychics, and visionaries have been doing for thousands of years. All you're doing is reclaiming a human ability that technology has derailed.
4. Try tape recording your meditation-visualization. Speak slowly, inserting pauses periodically to give yourself time to translate what you're hearing into a mental image. If you find the sound of your own voice distracting, ask a friend to do this for you.
5. Don't expect too much from yourself too soon. No one becomes a master of any magical technique in a day, and sometimes not in a lifetime. Go at your own pace.

Great Expectations

I love speaking at gatherings and listening to people's accounts of what happened after a particular prayer or meditation. They often muse about how oddly the universe interpreted a request, or how the insights from the meditation manifested outwardly. This is very normal, and I highly recommend putting this little note somewhere in your spellbook where you'll see it regularly:

Be careful what you wish for—you might get it
(but not the way you expect).
The Universe knows how to smile and laugh.
It endeavors to teach us to do likewise,
often by laughing at ourselves!

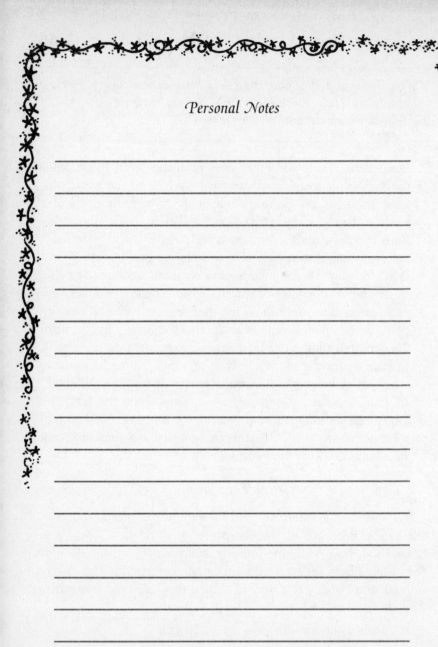

Personal Notes

_____

_____

_____

_____

_____

_____

_____

_____

_____

_____

_____

_____

_____

_____

_____

3

Sacred Space: Creating and Maintaining

Some of the most interesting reading you'll find in nearly any book on magic is the section about creating sacred space. The vivid invocations and prescribed movements are each so unique, creative, and inspired that it makes you want to pick up a pen and write some yourself. When you come across these kinds of spirit-guided invocations, by all means copy them into your Book of Shadows, then write out one or two of your own beneath! Let the encouraging energy in the words fill your pen and subsequently the pages of your spellbook.

The purpose of this section is to help you do just that. What I'm providing here are some simple constructs and neat ideas for sacred space workings. You can certainly use this information as it stands, but it might not be suited to your path. Instead, I recommend reviewing these ideas as an inspirational nudge to finding novel approaches for creating and maintaining sacred space. Next, adapt what's given here or create totally new methods so they truly synchronize with your magical tradition and vision. The resulting adaptations should then be transferred into your formalized Book of Shadows. Cross-reference these ideas with the Wheel of Life section too, since invocations are part of all ritual work.

What Constitutes Sacred Space

Before making notes on how to create a sacred space, it helps to
have a good idea of *what,* exactly, sacred space is. For some people, images of great cathedrals or graveyards come to mind. Thank-
fully, magical sacred space need not be that grandiose or gloomy.
I'm sure there have been moments in your life when you've gone
into a building or walked through a tract of land and noticed that
it felt different. There was a tingling in the air and a warm, vital
presence. This is a pretty good indication that you've stumbled
onto a specially designated or naturally occurring sacred space!

Really, any spot can become a sacred space if you think of it as
such, and treat it with appropriate respect. This is what I consider
informal sacred space. It is a holiness established by attitude, action,
and sometimes the addition of symbolic objects for support. For
example, your body is a sacred space unto itself, but you might wear
a crystal to improve your auric energies and provide a little more
spiritual confidence. Or, you might have special decorations around
your living area that, each time you see them, make you feel safe and
whole in the sacred space called home. I'll cover more ideas along
these lines under "Instant Sacred Space" later in this section.

In magical traditions, however, creating formalized sacred space
is a little different and a little more involved (See page 27, Seven
Steps for Creating Sacred Space). The intention is to put a spiritual
shield of force in place that keeps the raised energy safely within
until it's time to guide it elsewhere. This shield has a specific res-
onance that also keeps out any unwanted influences too. In effect,
this manifested force of will marks the line between the temporal
and spiritual world, between time and infinity.

Most formalized sacred spaces are designed to last for the dura-
tion of a particular working. The process is begun at the outset of
a ritual (or other magical protocol) by setting up an altar at a central point and some type of physical or mental circumference for
the circle around this point. Sometimes four mini-altars are set up
at due north, south, east, and west with symbolic tokens (like colored candles) on top.

Observation: This timeless quality of sacred space is why you'll often notice Wiccans taking off their watches before this entire procedure. Unless you have pressing time constraints, you might want to take the cue and do likewise. In fact, prior to creating a sacred space, the practitioners may have taken a special bath to purify their auras, meditated, fasted, or prayed to emphasize leaving behind worldly things and really prepare their spirits for magic. You may want to include these ideas in the ritual portion of your spellbook.

Frequently the designated area is cleansed before or during the ritual using sage smoke, an asperger, washing with lemon water, or other purifying items. This is simply a way of banishing any residual negativity or unwanted energy before the sacred powers are called into play. Just as you want to be ready physically, mentally, and spiritually for magical work, the area you work in should also be made ready.

Next, someone invokes protective elemental powers, called the Quarters or Watchtowers. (These are two terms you might want to add to your glossary, and you'll see several examples of solidly designed invocations you can use as patterns in the Wheel of Life section of this book.) The word Quarter refers to the fact that the directional wheel is divided into four main sections, each of which has an elemental correspondence (Earth-north, Fire-south, Water-west, Air-east). *Hint*: Copy these correspondences into the elements section of your spellbook.

The term Watchtower implies something more. See, each element has indwelling spirits that can be called upon to create and protect the sacred space. In other words, they "watch" over it and help guide the magic within. More on this subject will be covered under chapter 8, Elements, Correspondences, and Applications.

Generally invocations start in the east, which is the point of beginning (i.e., dawn) and end in the north moving clockwise. The clockwise movement is meant to follow the sun, which motivates positive energy and blessings. The only time one moves counterclockwise around the magic circle is for banishing, diminishing, or dismissing. *Hint:* You might want to copy this information into the Wheel of Life section of your spellbook. You can also use it in food and beverage magic by stirring or passing edibles clockwise!

At each point of the circle, the person reciting the invocation stops, welcomes the Guardians of that Quarter, and signifies their presence somehow. This indication can be the lighting of a candle, drawing a magical sigil in the air, putting out a symbol of the element, or other such actions. (Note: This also honors the presence of the Guardians). The practitioner might also, at this point, verbalize the purpose of the circle so the devic-elemental beings charge the area with harmonious energy.

Finally the invocation is completed by moving to a central point (the altar, a ritual fire, or whatever) and welcoming Spirit. This is the binding tie for all the elements and the spark for magic. In other words, this final part of the invocation equates to an opening prayer in other religious settings.

At the end of a circle procedure this entire process is reversed with similar elegance, or sometimes in an abbreviated format. The type of approach that is used often depends on time constraints or the type of magical process undertaken. For example, if one called upon a spirit or devic entity for assistance with something, both the invocation and dismissal will be more elaborate as a precaution. The rule of "safety first" applies with mystical methodology too!

Custom Designing Sacred Space

With all that said and done, there's nothing in my rule book that says you can't personalize the way you physically and psychically establish sacred space. If you're looking for some creative alternatives to keep in your Book of Shadows for those moments when ideas seem wanting, here are several:

Altar Variations

In section 1 you learned that people get really creative with their magical tools. So why not consider getting equally creative with your altar placement? While there are some people who insist altars *must* go in the east, I think there are many times when alternative placement makes perfect sense including:

- Putting the altar in the south for Fire-solar festivals, or when working magic for passion, energy, and purification.
- Putting the altar in the west come springtime to honor the Water element, or when working magic for rain, healing, inspiration, and for any lunar observances.
- Putting the altar in the north on Earth Day, or when working magic for grounding, security, finances, and other "earthly" matters.

Note: You might want to cross-reference this information in the Wheel of Life section of your spellbook.

Another way of making things a little more personal is with your choice of altar decorations. During spring observances, for example, I often forego a cauldron filled with water and fill a huge basket with spring flowers instead. These get strewn, in part, to mark the edge of the circle (See also "Circle Designation" section on page 70). I also try to find a way to incorporate them into a spell or activity suited to spring, like tossing some on running water while making a wish for abundance. *Hint:* Copy this last idea into the spells section of your Book of Shadows.

In choosing, adapting, or adding to your altar decorations consider the following:

- What items do you need at hand to complete the magical procedure, and do you want to change these at all? Substitutions are fine as long as they maintain a congruity of theme.
- What items suit the season or timing of the ritual?
- What items or symbols do you personally connect with the theme of this procedure, and can you add them to your embellishments somehow?
- How much space do you have available, and what decorations are safe considering that space? For example, if you have a very

small area it's not wise to have a lot of open flames; use self-contained candles instead.

• Is your altar's surface out of reach of children and/or pets? From my experience both pets and kids *love* magical energy and are drawn to it like a magnet. So, if either can reach your altar, keep whatever you put there safe for little hands and paws.

• If holding your procedure outdoors, what decorations will be best if it rains, gets windy, or other weather situations arise?

Remember that you have a lot of options to use in fulfilling the above guidelines. You can change the colors of the candles or altar cloth, the type of incense used, assemble some potted plants or freshly picked greenery, sprinkle some glitter around, find fun statues, or whatever. To give you a functional illustration, for lunar-related procedures I like to use a silvery satin altar cloth dusted with white or silver glitter. When you add white, lighted candles to this blend, the surface of the altar looks amazing and really feels more magical (to me, at least). And, really that's what all these extra touches are for—they help create a magical ambiance and mood that helps the entire process flow more easily.

Elemental Markers

If you plan on marking your magic circle at the four Quarters, your options are nearly endless in terms of objects to represent the elements. All the same considerations, as those for the altar's surface, apply to these objects, with the additional necessity that the item somehow symbolizes the correct element for the Quarter in which it's placed. Here are some examples of creative elemental markers:

EARTH   A globe, an atlas, the television (or computer), a green marble, a sprouting onion or potato from your vegetable bin

AIR   A fan or air conditioner, an open window, air freshener stick, feather duster, a child's airplane

FIRE Your fireplace, a stove or furnace pilot, a match, a toy fire truck, a lamp (turned on), sun catchers, a flashlight

WATER The sink or bathtub, a garden hose, a sprinkler can, your favorite coffee cup, the teakettle (this might be fire/water combined)!

Hint: Copy the above options into the elemental correspondence listings in your spellbook

Varying Quarter Correspondences

There has been a fair amount of discussion about varying the elemental correspondence of a particular Quarter to better suit your living environment. For example, if you live just east of a pond, lake, or river, east might become the Water center for your circle. Or, if you are south of a dormant volcano, the Fire element is geographically north!

I personally feel making these kinds of adjustments equates to a Wiccan version of Feng Shui. By so doing we're honoring the lay (and ley) of the land, and nature's symbolic markings. By extension, if you have a predominant plant in the eastern part of your home, this point might represent the Earth element instead of Air, just as a fireplace in the north part of your home can represent the Fire element. It's all in the way you look at it!

Starting/Ending Invocations in a Different Quarter

As I mentioned earlier this section, most invocations start in the eastern Quarter of the circle to represent beginnings. But just as it sometimes make more sense to designate the Quarters of your circle with nontraditional elemental correspondences, it also sometimes makes sense to begin invocations in a different quarter than usual. For example, while you can certainly start a solstice ritual in the east to honor the rising sun and dawn, you could also start the invocation due south, representing the sun in its fullness of power! Similarly, lunar-related activities might include invocations that begin in the west, with the Water element that ties to the moon.

So, when you read over any precreated rituals, spells, and other magical procedures that include invocations, keep this in mind. If you feel strongly that a particular element is better suited to set the tone for the entire activity, begin your invocation in the corresponding section instead, proceeding clockwise around the circle to the other quarters from that point. If the adaptation is successful, make notes of it in your Magical Diary, or in conjunction with that procedure in your Book of Shadows.

Circle Designation

In much the way you adorned your altar with personal touches, you can designate the perimeter of your circle with significant markers that are (a) visually appealing, (b) thematically appropriate, and (c) magically charged with energy to mark the line between the worlds. Earlier in this chapter I talked about using flower petals in this way, but that's only the beginning! Here are a few other fun ideas for you to try:

Balloons   Birthday gatherings and other celebratory festivals. *Note:* Put a little piece of masking tape beneath each balloon to keep them in place.

Beans   Divination efforts, hope-oriented magic. Use mixed beans, or those of a color suited to your goals.

Books   Study circles, spells-rituals-meditations for internalizing knowledge. Choose the titles according to the topic.

Branches (fallen, small)   Greenwood festivals, winter observances. Consider matching the type of branch to the theme of the activity, like oak for strength and pine for longevity. *Hint:* Copy these correspondences into the plant section of your spellbook.

Curled Ribbons   Beltane, cycle observances. Again, choose colors suited to the occasion and braid a few to represent life's network and our magical connections.

Glow-in-the-Dark Stars   Universal awareness, wish magic. You
can find these at gift shops and science stores and also use them
to decorate the altar, your ritual robe, or whatever!

Leaves   Autumn rites, harvest festivals.

Milk   Fertility rites, womanhood observances, blessingways. If
you don't want to make a mess, buy a bunch of single-serving
milk cartons and place them at equal intervals.

Seeds   Fertility spells, growth-related magic, spring observances.
In this case choose the type of plant seed according to its meta-
physical associations (refer to that section in your Book of
Shadows for ideas).

Torches   Outdoor gatherings for Candlemas or other Fire festivals-
observances. For the fun of it, find suitably scented torch oil.

Rice (colored or plain)   Weather spells, prosperity magic, providence rituals, harvest rites.

It's a good idea to cross-reference this information in the "Wheel
of Life" section of your Book of Shadows

Portable Sacred Space

This is a neat magical recipe that I only recently added to my
personal Book of Shadows. Since we live in a very mobile, transitory society sometimes we need portable sacred space. In this
case, rather than an area surrounded by a sphere of power
you'll be making an object whose protective sphere can be activated by your will or words. To make this object, you'll need a
small sealable container, some ashes from a magical fire (i.e.,
any fire previously used for ritual or spellcraft from which you
can gather ashes), a feather, a crystal or tiny stone, and a
seashell or sand.

Take the container and components beneath a full moon (or a
window where moonlight shines in). Put the ashes in the container saying,

"Spirit of Fire, I conjure and call you. Leave a small spark of your power in this object to protect and energize my sacred space wherever I may be. Come to life when I say _____."

Fill in the blank with a word or activating phrase that you can easily remember. (Repeat this procedure with the other elemental tokens, changing the name of the spirit called accordingly.) Close up the container, and invoke your patron or patroness to bless your efforts and bind the magic within.

Make as many of these as you need for your car or cars, briefcase, purse, suitcase, or whatever. Whenever you want to activate the object, hold it in both hands, center yourself, and whisper the activating phrase three times with purpose. Visualize a bright white light radiating outward with you in the center. This sphere of force will remain in effect until you release it by speaking the activating phrase a fourth time. Why use the numbers three and four? Three is the number of body-mind-spirit working in harmony. The fourth repetition grounds the energy, being the number of Earth. *Hint:* Copy these extra correspondences for three and four into the color-sound-texture-number section of your spellbook.

You may find these portable sacred spaces need to be replaced periodically. Like a fetish, there's a limited amount of energy you can store in them, and a limited number of times you can recharge them. When you feel the token has lost its capacity to hold energy effectively, dispose of it ritually (bury, burn, or throw it in running water) and make a new one.

"Instant" Sacred Space

Along the same lines of portable sacred space, our lives are often too busy to allow for long, drawn-out rituals. There are also occasions when immediacy of need takes priority over formality. That's when you can use the idea of informal sacred space as a foundation, with a little twist learned from making portable sacred space!

Find four everyday objects in your home that you can use to represent the elements. Put each object at (or near) the correct directional center for its element. As you put the object in place adapt the invocation used previously to something like,

> *"Spirit of _____, I call and charge you to fill this token. Radiate _____ (a characteristic attribute of the element, like love for Fire) through my sacred space of home, and fill it with your protective energy when I say _____."*

As before fill in the last blank with an easily remembered word or phrase. Then when you need to set up sacred space quickly, just point to the object and speak the word or phrase three times. Leave the sacred space firmly in place until you feel safe again, or you're done with the magic at hand, then dismiss it with the fourth repetition and a few words of thanks.

Word of Advice: Always remember to say thank you to the powers for their presence and help. A thankful heart is one ready to both give and receive.

Maintaining Informal Sacred Space

This section is very important especially for those of you who live in urban environments. Urbania barrages our sacred spaces with noise and crowded conditions. This means that the objects you've put in place for informal, ongoing protection will need regular care and maintenance to continue functioning really well. Here's how:

- Regularly purify the items. This can be accomplished by soaking them in lemon water, burying them in salt, smudging them with sage, or the like.
- Charge up the items by sunlight and moonlight for a balance of masculine-feminine, intuitive-logical energies.
- Keep the items clean in between purifications and chargings (i.e., dust free).
- Replace any item that gets broken with something suitable and new. Repeat the process of giving the token an activating phrase,

and continue around the circle to the others, so the four items work harmoniously together.

Remember, there is no right or wrong time to create sacred space. Folk magicians often cast spells without establishing a formal sacred space first, while ritual magicians will rarely do so. The final decision is up to you. While it might not *always* be necessary, it is *always* helpful to make a protected sphere within which your magic can grow and develop unhindered.

Suggested Reading

Wiccan Book of Ceremonies and Rituals. Patricia Telesco. Secaucus, N.J.: Carol Publishing Group, 1998.

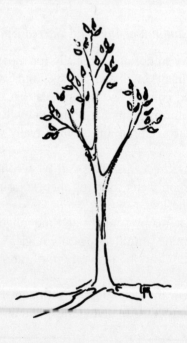

Personal Notes

_____

_____

_____

_____

_____

_____

_____

_____

_____

_____

_____

_____

_____

_____

_____

_____

_____

_____

4

Spells and Spell Components

The easiest way to think about this section of your Book of Shadows is to compare it to a family cookbook. Here you'll be recording all the best recipes for manifesting your magical goals. You'll also be noting any variations on tried-'n'-true recipes that you found particularly useful and effective. Before you begin, however, the first step is appraising your magical ingredients and their symbolic value.

Spell Components

Spell components are the ingredients that you will choose, measure, and blend into harmonious magical energy. And unlike some of the depictions of a Witch using unsavory components, there's nothing about modern magical spell components that's odd, icky, or vulgar. In fact, folk magic advocates the use of ingredients that are readily available in, and around, your living space!

Surprised? So was I. Even more so when I realized that there's nothing on this planet that can't potentially be used as a spell component, focus, or prop including rubber bands, the microwave, and your socks! (See the Spell Methodology section on page 80.)

Want to know my secrets for making anything work as an effective spell component? You can find many of them in my book *Spinning Spells, Weaving Wonders* (Freedom, CA: Crossing Press, 1996), and the rest are here! If they make sense to you, copy this chart into your spellbook.

KEY TO COMPONENT COMPETENCY

1. Stop thinking of things as just physical in nature. All things have an astral presence too. In that presence, and its symbolic value, lies its magical potential.
2. Don't be restricted by right-brain thinking. Get creative with your component choices, using what's handy and meaningful (including *you*).
3. Consider what the item is used for normally. How does that use translate into magic? For example, we use the microwave to speed up cooking? Well, couldn't it likewise speed up the manifestation of our magic?

Hint: Copy or cross-reference this last idea into the food and beverage section of your spellbook.

4. Try several different spell methods, mixtures, and goals using that item as a central component. Challenge yourself to find ten different applications for the item in your spellcraft and make notes of the most successful applications in your Book of Shadows.
5. Be patient. It's often hard for us to get past the temporal self and see the possibilities in items that we associate with mundanity. Good old trial and error can be a great teacher and a wonderful medium for amazing discoveries.
6. Use only those things that have the right symbolism for helping achieve your goals, specifically items that you immediately connect with the theme of that goal. Not to do so is like using flour instead of sugar in your "recipe"—it just won't bake right.
7. Finally, remember that nothing is too silly or simple to work effectively if it's meaningful to you, if you remain resolute, and if you trust in your magic.

Okay, so now you know how I choose many spell components. I also keep lists of traditional correspondences in my spellbook to refer to in the consideration process. These are especially useful with things like herbs, crystals, and colors that have had metaphysical associations ascribed to them for hundreds of years. There's a certain strength in beliefs that have been repeated, handed down, and applied for a long time. The power of communal faith is something that you should never underestimate in your magic. So, if there's a more traditional spell component that can be used to achieve your goals, and it makes sense to you, by all means use it and include it in your Book of Shadows!

All I'm trying to discourage here is the tendency toward using rote spell instructions without having a personal connection to the process or components represented, and without thinking seriously about the process. This is my personal spellcraft mantra, and one I think about regularly:

Personalize, Feel It, Be It!

Categorizing Spell Components

With that bit of soapboxing out of the way, let's go on to looking at good ways of organizing the spell components you decide to list in your Book of Shadows. There are a couple of effective ways to approach this, and actually I use all three. The first is a simple alphabetical listing set up something like the abbreviated chart that follows. (The alphabetical list format has many potential applications.) If you have space, you might want to add some neat historical-folkloric information on the items you work with most often. *Hint:* Copy the applications you don't already have into your spellbook for future reference.

Component	Element	Applications
Amethyst	Water	Regulating emotions, dreams
Bottles, Jars	Varies	Protection, wishes
Cinnamon	Fire	Energy, passion, love

Note: Cinnamon was favored as a temple herb for anointing, offerings, and incense!

Door	Earth	Beginnings, ending, welcome
Egg	Spirit	Fruitfulness, creativity, hope, healing

Note: In some creation myths the universe and certain deities were birthed from an egg (*Cross-reference with food-beverage section of your spellbook*).

Feather	Air	Divination, wish magic
Gum	Earth	Adhering to beliefs
Honey	Air	Joy, offerings, health
Jade	Water	Abundance, love, weather magic
Milk	Water	Goddess, maternal nature

Note: Milk was once considered a suitable offering to the gods, and it has strong lunar energies (*Cross-reference this with the food-beverage part of your spellbook*).

Oven	Fire	Love, warmth, closure
Pen	Air	Powerful communication
Radish	Fire	Protection, overcoming
Scissors	Fire	Separation, cutting away
Telephone	Air	Communication, messages
Walnut	Fire	God, the mind, safety
Yarn	Earth	Binding/releasing, web weaving

The second approach is to have separate lists by theme. Using the above list as a starting point, these lists might look something like this, with more additions as time goes on:

Communication	*Love*	*Wishes*
Pen	Oven	Bottles
Telephone	Jade	Feathers
	Cinnamon	

The third approach is to have separate alphabetized lists by component category, like crystals, vegetables, herbs, and the like.

Good examples of this organizational method can be seen throughout the rest of this Book of Shadows, specifically chapters 9, 10,
11, and 12.

CHALLENGE

Take one month during which you make a list of all the everyday items in your house including the food in your refrigerator,
spices on the shelf, odds and ends in the sewing box, and the
like. Afterward, create your own magical correspondence list
from this inventory, using personal insights, folklore, myths, history, and any traditional mystical applications you can find.
Transfer the items you think you'll use most often to your spellbook. I promise you'll never look at your living space the same
way again!

Spell Methodology

A whole bunch of really fine ingredients won't do you much good
if you don't have a recipe to follow, at least when you're first learning to cook. Spells are like that, too. There are methods and means
to blending spells together so that the energy created manifests in
the best possible way. This section reviews some of the common
spell methodologies that I have personally found to be effective.
Read through this information, see what helps the most, and what
works best for you, then transfer those suggestions and ideas into
your Book of Shadows.

Determining Goals and Time Frames

Spells are will-driven mechanisms, so it's very important that
you have a clearly defined goal before you start putting ingredients
together. Any uncertainty or mental murkiness will deter, if not
totally derail, the magic you hope to make. In defining your goal,
make sure to give it as much form and dimension as possible. Consider things like:

- What effect do you want this spell to have over time?
- Who or what is this energy intended to affect?
- Why exactly is the spell being cast? (Understanding your intention often thwarts knee-jerk reactions when you're angry or frustrated.)
- When do you need the spell to manifest?

Once you have your goal and its facets firmly established in your mind and spirit, you can then consider timing. While the specifics of magical timing is better covered in chapter 6, "The Wheel of Life," it has bearing on spellcraft, too. So you may want to cross-reference these sections in your Book of Shadows, or copy the information that you feel is most pertinent in both places.

In brief, choosing auspicious timing provides a cosmic boost to the power and the manifesting accuracy of a spell. Think of this as connecting the strands of your magic to a jumper cable. The magic has power by itself, but the energy coursing through the cables (provided by the proper placement of the planets, sun, moon, and stars), increases that energy geometrically. So, while I've always been one to believe that any time is the right time for magic, adding symbolic timing certainly can't hurt. *Hint:* When you're thinking about magic, consider how immediate your needs are. If a spell or ritual can be put off for more beneficial astrological timing, then wait. Let the universe help you in any way possible.

Choice and Use of Focals and Props

Just like cooking requires certain tools to help the process along, spellcraft also has implements, specifically focals and props. And, just like your components, there's no limit to the variety of implements available.

Beginning with focals, this is an item that directs your whole attention to the matter at hand. Probably the most common magical focal that comes to mind is a candle flame. Here, a practitioner fixes his or her gaze on the focal, breathing deeply, and slowly letting the rest of the world disappear. During this time, his or her mind also shifts to the matter at hand.

The kinds of focals that work best for each person vary. Usually a focal that (a) represents your goal somehow and draws your attention to it, or (b) has sensual appeal, is also one that will work effectively for you. For example, a person strongly affected by sound might use music as a means of fixing their concentration. Someone who finds aromas evocative might burn incense and find that it shifts their awareness. Or, someone who responds to movement might dance a pantomime of their spell's energy taking form in real life. This is a kind of sympathetic magic that works very well in a ritual or meditative context, too. It's based on the law of like effecting like. Imitating your magic as already manifested sets up the vibration of success.

Empowering Words and Writings

If you review the magical methods from places as culturally diverse as Egypt and Scotland, you'll notice something interesting. While the components they used for magic often differed, certain methods were a lot alike. For the modern practitioner this means two things. First, that there is a universal theme to magic that goes beyond time, culture, and society. Second, there are core techniques for magic that are considered invaluable. Verbal and written spells are among those universal methods.

Verbal and written spells have a few elements in common, namely repetition and rhyme. Rhyme was used as a mnemonic device that also moved the practitioner toward a more meditative state (it still can be used this way). Repetition served two other functions. The number of repetitions were often symbolic (such as repeating two incantations in a spell focused on partnership, or writing two verses and carrying them with you as part of a spell for personal balance). Reiterating or rewriting the spell also increased the active magical power in it. *Hint:* When you can't recite an incantation out loud, recite it in your mind; let the energy of thought guide your magic!

Written spells added yet another dimension, that of a meaningful visual form. Perhaps the most well known of these kinds of spells is the ancient "abracadabra." The word itself translates as something like "to diminish," and traditionally abracadabra is written in the form of a decreasing triangle (point down). Once the symbol is written down, the practitioner is supposed to bury it or place it in a tree so that sickness will wane like the word itself shrinks! *Note:* This is another excellent example of sympathetic-imitative magic, which may provide whole new magical dimensions for artistic people to explore, like painting an ever-growing pile of money over several weeks as part of a prosperity spell!

As you can see with abracadabra, written spell forms need not be limited to words. Shapes or symbols are useful, too. The key here is focusing your will and purposefully drawing the chosen emblem so that it's filled with magical energy. Usually once the magic from such an item has manifested, it's respectfully destroyed by burying or burning it in a ritual fire.

So in your Book of Shadows, make notes of the incantations you find most useful (or adaptable), and sketch out any written or symbolic spells that you like. When a specific verbal or written form works well for you, use it regularly for similar goals. (As the old saying goes, if it's not broke, don't fix it!) Also, see if there might be ways you can tweak it for different needs and aims.

Adding Visualization or Symbolic Actions

Visualizations and physical actions can help your spellcasting tremendously. Visualization gives a mental form to your goal. This form allows you to relate to your goal more effectively than you would to an amorphous, passing thought. Also, in magic, if you can imagine it as *real* it will be easier for the energy to manifest in reality.

Actions work in a similar way. A lot of people forget that their body is a tool, too. I've already talked about mimicry as a potent method for magic, but here are a few more examples to keep in mind: pointing is an effective way of directing energy, releasing hands upward can guide a cone of power, rising from the floor slowly helps physically express growth oriented magic, and so forth.

What's important for your Book of Shadows is to maintain notes of what imagery and actions helped a specific type of spell. This information may also prove useful in a ritual construct, since rituals are basically elongated spells with other elements added to improve the meaning for all participants. The only difference between verbal and written components for a group and those for the individual is that the group should recite incantations together to unite their wills, and written forms need to be large enough or plentiful enough to guide everyone's focus.

Repetition to Build Supportive Power

Some people only cast a spell once, feeling that they should trust the procedure, the magic it created, and the universe for manifestation. Other people like to repeat spells regularly until they come to fruition, feeling that each time a spell's enacted it focuses more power toward the goal.

Exactly which method you choose for spellcraft, and to include in your Book of Shadows, is purely personal. There is no right or wrong answer other than what your heart says to do. There are times when you'll cast a spell and just know the energy hit its mark (I can't explain this, but you will know). There are other times when things seem uncertain or "off." These are the occasions when repetition builds more personal confidence and faith, which is important to manifestation, too. Besides that, repeating the spell gives the original energy a little extra nudge in the right direction.

Divine Blessings

If you follow a god or goddess (or even if you have a generic designation for this power), it never hurts to ask for that Power's blessing on your spellcraft. Since human beings are mortal, we have a limited capacity to see the extended effects of our spellcraft. The god/dess, however, can see the entire picture. So, by asking the god/dess to step in and guide the energy beneficially, we avoid magical errors that come out of human limitations and failings.

One thing along these lines that you may wish to put in your Book of Shadows is the phrase *"for the greatest good, and it harm none."* This is what I call the universal clause of ritual and spellcraft. When we release our magic followed by that phrase, we acknowledge the part of the spiritual equation that we cannot see, and ask that if we've erred that the Powers correct that error. This is one of the reasons that spellcraft doesn't always manifest in the way we expect—*"the greatest good"* isn't always what we think is good for us!

Sample Spells for Your Book of Shadows

Every Wiccan you meet will have spells that they favor. I'm no exception to this rule. So at this point I'd like to share with you four folk spells that I really like because they're pretty simple, highly adaptable, and very effective. If you like these, feel free to copy them into your spellbook for use later.

The String Spell

For the string spell you'll need a table-safe fire source (like a brazier), a piece of paper, and a three-foot length of string. On the piece of paper write out your goal (finding a lost object, increasing money flow, healing a relationship, or whatever). Fold the paper three times and tie it onto one end of the string. Put the fire source just in front of you on a table and the paper-bound end of the string across the table from you. Keep the other end of the string in your strong hand.

Now, take a deep breath and imagine your goal is being fulfilled. Very slowly draw the string toward you, continuing to focus your will wholeheartedly on manifestation saying, *"To me, to me, come to me."* When at last the paper reaches your hand, hold it tightly for a moment more and then toss it in the fire. As it burns, the energy you've created is released to begin working. Keep the ashes in a safe place until the spell has worked, then give them to the winds with thankfulness.

The Ice Spell

This spell is particularly useful when you want to slow down a situation that's moving too quickly (like a relationship), halt negativity, and create protection. Take an object that represents the person, animal, item, or situation you want to slow down, halt, or safeguard. If you can't find a small token, writing this information on paper works just as well.

Next, put the token or paper into an ice cube tray and pour water on top. Hold this in both hands directing your will into the water. If you wish, add an incantation or chant that describes your purpose. Put the container in the freezer.

Scientifically we know that water freezes because the cold slows down the molecules (thus the slowing of the situation). The hard surface halts negativity (and reflects it), and also protects what's inside from outside influences. Once the ice cube is frozen, pop it out and keep it in the back of your freezer until you feel the problem has passed, then give it to the earth.

Knot Spells

I love working knot magic because the symbolism of binding energy into the knot is so potent. For a knot spell you'll obviously need something that can be tied like a scarf, a swatch of fabric, rope, string, thread, a shoelace, or even a strand of your hair. *Hint:* Transfer these knotting ideas into your component list under creative alternatives! It's an extra bonus if the item somehow reflects the energy you plan to hold within it, like using a winter scarf to house a health spell.

Hold the item in your hands and think about your goal. Start tieing a knot (or a series of knots), whispering your goal into the binding eight times (this is the number of completion and fulfillment). Continue holding the item and pouring in energy until it's filled to overflowing. Then, when you need that spell released, slim-ply untie one knot. *Hint:* Copy or cross-reference the historical information on knot magic from page 41 here.

Mirror Spells

Mirrors reflect or redirect energy. I use them in protection spells and karmic reprisal spells. For the former, I simply empower a mirror with an incantation during a full moon and put it facing outward in a window. This reflects away any negativity. For the latter, I glue the name of the person I feel might be doing something against me face down on the mirror. This way, if they're not doing anything wrong, nothing whatsoever happens. If they are, whatever energy they send out is simply "returned to sender"!

Responsible Spellcraft

I know this has been said hundreds of times by hundreds of people, but I wouldn't be a good teacher if I didn't mention it again. Please be responsible with the kind of spells you keep in your Book of Shadows, and even more so with those you cast. Forcing people's wills, cursing people, and other negative intentions will only result in harm to you, too. This kind of magic reflects badly on the entire magical community and reinforces the stereotypical image of the "evil witch." Remember, there are magical measures for handling bad things in positive ways, like mirror spells. As long as you honestly *try* to keep your magic positive, the universe honors the intention of your heart.

Personal Notes

5

Charms, Amulets, Talismans, and Fetishes

Charms, amulets, talismans, and fetishes are basically portable spells. Considering how mobile and transitory our society has become, this kind of magic is among the most important to include in your Book of Shadows. In designing a section on portable magic, you'll want to make note of the process for making each item, what components you need, and how the completed item gets used. This chapter reviews some of this information as translated from my own Book of Shadows, and gives you a few examples to try. Copy them into your spellbook if they prove successful for you too.

Charms

The word charm comes from the Latin *carmen*, which means a poem or harmonic song. This connection may explain either why charm creation usually centers around an incantation, or why incantations have been an important part of spellcraft for so long. Hmm, chicken. . .egg?

Anyway, by definition a charm can be anything—an object, word, or symbol—that's believed to have inherent or given magical

powers. Charms can be designed for protection against sickness, to
turn mal-intent, and to encourage good luck, but most are created
to help with matters of the heart. Thus we come to the origins of
charm bracelets as a gift between lovers. Each token on the
bracelet represented hopes and feelings, and wearing the bracelet
was then thought to help encourage those things in the wearer's
life. Examples include:

anchor: stability	flower: hope, health
boat: travel, adventure	knot: promises
clover: luck	house: a happy home
heart: love	baby: children
shoe: fertility, abundance	coin: prosperity

Hint: Copy the above symbols into section 1 of your spellbook
along with others that you find useful.

Modern magicians use these concepts as a foundation, often
combining an incantation with a symbolic object for the finished
charm. Why? Because the verbalized element works in tandem
with the practitioner's will, wrapping the object in energy that
gets absorbed into its matrix. So, the magic actually changes the
charm's basic energy patterns to match the desired pattern (for
love, luck, or whatever). Charms are considered a kind of elementary magic, so the change that occurs usually isn't permanent. It's meant to last for a period of time, slowly releasing
energy like a time-released vitamin into, and around, the practitioner's life.

If the charm is designed to be wholly verbal or written, it works
a little differently. A verbal charm is recited at the moment when
the practitioner needs it to manifest. It's often repeated a symbolic
number of times to reemphasize the will of the practitioner and
support the vibrations of the incantation.

A written charm often has a symbolic shape (or color). For
example, a series of words might be written in the form of an
inward spiral to stress internalization of personal magic. Or, a
charm for luck might be written in green ink. Generally, activating
the charm only requires carrying it; however, if the charm consists

of a series of written words, the practitioner might repeat those words and touch the charm as a means of triggering it.

Sample Charms for Your Book of Shadows

Rose Quartz Charm

This is for gentle love, including self love. To energize this charm, hold it to your heart and visualize pink light pouring down from above you, through your heart, into the stone. As you do, whisper the word "love" continuously. When the quartz begins to feel hot or starts vibrating in your hands, it's ready to carry. This charm accents all kinds of love in your life (including the love of family and friends). If you put it under your pillow it also evokes dreams about loving relationships. *Hint:* Copy or cross-reference this idea into the crystal, metal, and mineral section of your spellbook.

Mirror Charm

This is for turning away negativity and unwanted magic. Begin with a small mirror (the size of a compact). Take some lipstick and draw a red X across the mirror while saying "*negativity away, all mischief at bay*." Wrap this in a white cloth so the lipstick doesn't smudge and carry it with you. This particular charm should be replaced regularly since it collects undesired vibrations into itself.

Coins of Fortune

To improve your overall serendipity, find a penny (preferably one minted in the year you were born). When you find it use the old childhood rhyme, "*See a penny pick it up, all the day you'll have good luck*" as the incantation to energize the charm. If you want the charm to last longer than twenty-four hours, watch for a silver-toned coin instead, and change "*day*" to "*month.*" I don't recommend using this particular charm for longer than one full moon cycle because silver is a lunar metal. For best results, however, the coin must be found by happenstance, not by hunting through your change.

Lucky Ash Leaf

A very old English charm begins by plucking an ash leaf and saying, "*Leaf of ash I do thee pluck, to bring to me a day of luck.*" This leaf is then carried for good fortune. *Hint:* Transfer this information about the ash tree into the plant correspondence list in your Book of Shadows.

Adapting this a bit, since many people wouldn't recognize an ash tree if it bit them, try this written charm instead. Take some wood ash (any kind) and write the word "luck" on a piece of paper using your index finger dipped in the soot. Fold this in on itself three times saying, "*Word of ash folded three by three, bring to me serendipity!*" Carry the charm frequently to manifest more luck in your life.

Amulets

The word amulet comes from the Latin *amuletum* meaning "a charm." So, you're immediately going to see some strong similarities between charms and amulets. The main difference between the two is that amulets are designed specifically to protect, preserve, and remedy. Also, traditional amulets were designed out of carved stones, shaped metals, or bundled plant matter rather than everyday objects. The reason for this difference was the belief that a precious base material absorbed and held more powerful magic. This is certainly food for thought to the modern practitioner. Cost doesn't always ensure quality, but there is something to be said for using the best components available to help achieve the best possible results.

Another interesting quirk about amulets is that the instructions for making them are often painstakingly precise about the order in which the base components are assembled. For example, an amulet for health might begin with a piece of copper (thought to have healing qualities) and a symbol for banishing (it's hard to get better if the spirit of sickness remains). *Hint:* Add this use for copper to your metals correspondence list.

The next symbol applied to the copper might be something representing rest, which is necessary to full recovery. A third emblem might be for ongoing protection so that once recovery is complete, the bearer stays well! In this manner the ancient magicians were teaching us that working with natural progressions (in this case turning illness to rest to recovery to protection) helps the magical process! *Note:* This works in spellcraft and rituals too!

Amulets can be worn, carried, placed among clothing, hung over doorways, put on animals, and even planted in soil to saturate a region with their powers.

> The Witch Bottle, a jar filled with sharp shards and urine or other repugnant components, is a good example of a regional amulet. It was traditionally buried near the threshold of a home to keep the house and lands safe from malevolent magic and ill fortune.

Sample Amulets for Your Book of Shadows

Water-Worn Stone Amulet

These protect relationships. For best results, keep the stone near the hearth (the heart of your home) or bound to a picture of the couple whose relationship you wish to protect. If the stone has a hole through it, hang it over the doorway to keep negativity outside and mischievous fairies at bay. *Hint:* Copy this last piece of information into your stone correspondence list.

Tree Amulet

By far the most popular of the ancient amulets were those fashioned from Mother Earth's storehouse. In India, a potent all-purpose amulet was created by gathering a piece of bark from the eastern side of ten different types of trees and binding them together with gold wire (*a solar symbol that should be added to your metal correspondences if it's not already there*). Inexpensive gold wire can be purchased at craft shops. I also recommend wrapping this entire bundle in white cloth to keep the bark from chipping. Put it where ongoing protective energy is needed most.

Anti-Magic Amulet

This amulet gathers elements recommended by mages in various cultures into one little bundle. You'll need a clove of garlic (Rome), a snapdragon or peony (Greece), an almond (Italy), and a washed peach stone (China), along with a piece of sturdy white cloth and a string. During a waning moon (to banish negativity) place the items in the cloth and tie them inside saying, *"Turn, turn, turn away. Any mal-intended magic, kept at bay."* Carry the bundle or keep it in your home.

Ring Amulets

It was a very common practice to make jewelry so that it not only decorated the body, but adorned the spirit. Copper, silver, gold, or iron rings repel sorcery. Copper also keeps sickness away, brass rings safeguard the wearer from ghostly visitations, and a ring made from a horseshoe nail turns away bad luck! If you want to use any of your personal rings for this purpose, the ring should be cleansed and blessed, then energized somehow. Use any methods suited to your path, then give the ring its purpose through willful visualization, an incantation, or an activating word as talked about in the section "Instant" Sacred Space (page 72).

Talisman

Amulets are considered passive protectors that simply radiate energy around the bearer no matter what. Amulets can be activated by the bearer, but they themselves are not "active" by nature. Talismans, by comparison, were once active participants in magic. For example, a magic wand became a talisman for transformative magic, as did the rod of Moses.

In folk stories most talismans are represented as having a kind of indwelling knowledge or soul. This indwelling energy can be communicated with (and appeased) for assistance. This spirit is often picky about its owner (e.g., the story of Aladdin's lamp, which could be acquired for free by a good-natured person, but had to be bought by someone evil), and the talisman may not function if the bearer gets into a tiff with the associated spirit or offends it somehow.

For example, say you had a talismanic staff with an indwelling earth deva. If you accidentally littered or committed some other offense toward the earth, your staff might suddenly stop working, or produce anything but what you hoped for magically. Mind you, this type of magic is rare these days because modern talismans have been confused with amulets and charms, the words regularly being used interchangeably.

Most contemporary magicians have gotten away from conjuring or capturing spirits into an object because of the dangers involved. So, what presently sets talismans apart from other portable magic is the inclusion of auspicious timing in their creation process and the nearly universal use of incantations to empower the object. Additionally, talismans often integrate figures of constellations or other sigils to portray the magic desired.

Sample Talismans for Your Book of Shadows

Bread Talisman

Bread makes an excellent talisman for providence and kinship. Begin by buying or baking a loaf of bread during a waxing to full moon. Folklore tells us that baking bread during this moon phase helps the loaf rise properly. *Hint:* Transfer this information into the food-beverage section of your spellbook. Take one slice from the bread. Dampen your pointer with a little water and write a symbol that somehow represents your need on the bread slice.

Remember to keep your goal in mind as you work, and add an incantation at this juncture that verbally supports that goal. Toast the bread to reveal manifested pattern. Wrap the bread carefully in a cloth and keep it somewhere safe (like the freezer). As long as the bread doesn't break or mold, it will release the energy you've placed within it.

Talisman of Finding

This talisman will help you find things be they lost, or simply something you've been unable to hunt down successfully. To begin, you will need a tiny three-pronged branch that's shaped like a capital Y. Go to a nearby park and hunt around (check bushes too—these yield smaller pieces). You want one that can easily be carried with you.

Once you find the branch, wait until the moon is in Libra to create the talisman. During this moon sign, wrap the long end of the Y-shaped branch with a braided strand of yellow, purple, and white string or yarn (these represent spirit, communication, and pure intention). As you tie this in place, add an incantation like "*When I hold you in my hand, let nothing from me hide.*" Then whenever you're searching for something, grasp the talisman, close your eyes, and think of the thing you want to find. See what mental images or physical signals you receive (like suddenly feeling drawn to a particular direction or store).

> *Neat Bit of Information:* The design of this talisman is based on the shape of traditional dowsing rods, which were once called Water Witching Sticks!

Key of Opening Talisman

This talisman is designed to help create opportunities for the bearer, and a smooth path wherever he or she goes. As such, it's an excellent item to keep in your car, brief case, or other similar places. Begin with an old skeleton key and a goodly length of rainbow-colored ribbon. The rainbow represents hope, while the ribbon symbolizes the magical network of life. *Hint:* Copy these to your list of symbols.

Wait until April or when the moon is in Aries. Go out under the noonday sun and twist the ribbons together. (Recognizing opportunity when it knocks is a function of the conscious mind, which is governed by the sun.) Slide these through the top of the key so you can hang it somewhere, or wear it. If you wish, add an incantation at this point. Repeat the incantation and touch the key any time you really need help in finding a quicker way to achieve a goal or resolve a problem.

Fetish

The word "fetish" appears in a variety of languages. In Portuguese, for example, it is *feitico*, meaning "to contrive a charm." Through this definition we see that this type of portable magic is intricately connected with the others covered in this section.

A fetish can be nearly anything that the bearer regards as being representative of a power, specifically a deity or demigod. By this definition, a statue of the Virgin Mary adorned with rosaries in the home of a Catholic could be considered in this category. And, while most mainstream Christians would shudder at the idea, a cross or Bible held for protection has strong connections with this type of portable magic.

Fetishes can also be any object to which you have a strong emotional reaction. If, for example, you see a picture of a little kitten and it arouses warm, happy feelings, this picture could become a fetish for joy and emotional warmth. The only real difference is that you regard the object differently, knowing that it inspires a certain magic in your heart.

Sample *Fetishes* for *Your* Book of Shadows

Fetishes can be designed to be "one use" items, or for long-term effects. One use fetishes have a very specific intention, often being burned, buried, tossed in running water, or scattered to the wind to bring about manifestation.

Negativity Fetish

Say you want a fetish that will remove the negativity you're carrying toward an individual or a situation. The perfect medium to use for this is a picture of that person, or perhaps a business card, since it evokes a strong emotional response. Go with that feeling, tear up the chosen representative, and then burn it to release the ties and the negative feelings.

Blessing Fetish

This you'll want to be a long-term fetish, so using a god or goddess image is a good place to start. Regularly leave offerings by this image to indicate a respectfulness for the power-persona represented. In turn, the fetish continually blesses your home. When you have very specific needs, change your offerings to mirror those needs, like leaving a few coins for improved cash flow.

For those of you with neoshamanic leanings, you can find wonderful animal carvings at nature stores to use as fetishes instead. In this case the representation disperses energy suited to that animal's attributes.

Portable Magic as Gift Items

Charms, amulets, talismans, and fetishes make lovely, thoughtful gifts *but* the recipient should always know what it is they've received. If possible, explain the significance of each part of the token. (Remember, understanding builds meaning, which is the heart of magic.) If the intended recipient isn't of a magical persuasion, I recommend sticking to amuletic work (which is passive), and explaining that you made it based on the folklore associated with that individual's need. In this manner you've made it more user friendly and less "hocus pocus."

Suggested Reading

Goddess in My Pocket. Patricia Telesco. San Francisco: Harper-Collins, 1998.

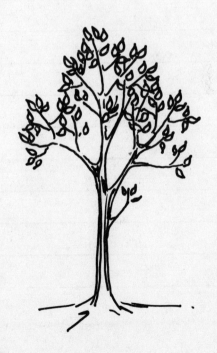

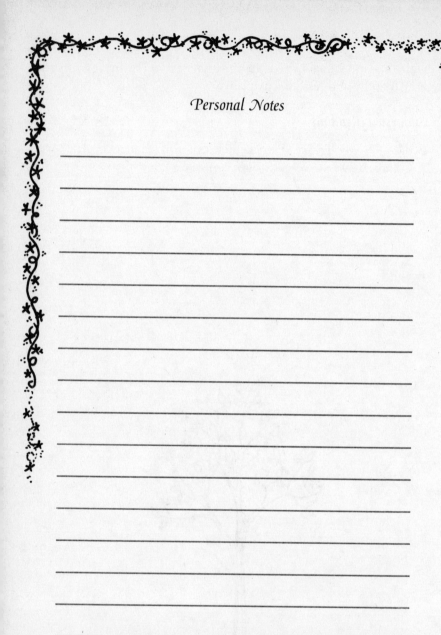

Personal Notes

6

The Wheel of Life

This part of your Book of Shadows is dedicated to time in all its forms: the hours of the day, the days of the week, the months, moon phases, the seasons, and the turning of the years. Wiccans regard time as circular, taking a cue from the cycles we see represented in nature. The sun rises, sets, and returns. The moon waxes, wanes, sleeps, and returns. The seasons return. These are the cycles that Wiccan ritual honors in both personal and planetary ways.

In a book of this size, I won't be able to give you a lot of rituals to transfer into your spellbook. What I can do, instead, is give you some ideas that facilitate ritual planning, creation, and adaptation.

Timing

Every moment of every day holds unique magical potential. For thousands of years mages have watched the Sun, the Moon, and the stars to determine the best time to cast a spell or hold an observance. Over time, certain rituals became customary in their timing, like those for the seasons or those that commemorated important community events. Other rituals, however, remained linked to specific astrological events, the practitioner waiting until the heavens and Earth synchronized with their magical goal.

These days "need" rarely has patience as a virtue, and our schedules don't always allow for detailed time constraints. Nonetheless, when your agenda does allow it, timing your rituals for auspicious hours, days, months, moon signs, and the like certainly can help with successful, potent manifestation. How do you choose among the options? Good question. The best answer is that you try to use them all, if possible (finding the right moon sign, during the right month, on the right day, at the right hour). This can get very complex, as you might imagine. So the second best option is to put as many positive factors together as possible.

To do that you'll need some correspondence lists in your Book of Shadows, and a decent astrological calendar to which to refer. I'm going to provide some sample lists that will get this section in your spellbook started, but you'll probably want to do more research into timing symbolism for greater detail. For the calendar, I recommend Llewellyn's annual Witches' calendar. It provides moon signs, lunar phases, auspicious colors, holidays, astrological signs, sun signs, planetary motion, and planting and harvesting days to help you along. (Call Llewellyn Publications at 1-800-843-6666 for more information.)

WEEKDAYS AND ASSOCIATIONS

Hint: Copy some of this information into the god-goddess section of your spellbook under attributes.

MONDAY   Monday gets its name from the Moon, so it's not surprising that this day rules over lunar matters including instinctiveness, psychic gifts, the maternal nature, and water magic.

TUESDAY   Tuesday gets its name from the Scandinavian god Tyr who presided over laws and athletics. His name also means "council." Tuesday influences matters of physical and mental activity, including reasoning and advice.

WEDNESDAY   Wednesday was named after the Germanic god Odin (Wotan to the Teutons), who presided over magic, the muse, and shrewdness. Wednesday therefore influences creativity, innovation, occult studies, and psychic insight.

THURSDAY   Thursday is Thor's day. In Scandinavian tradition, Thor was a kindly god who ruled the weather, blessed marriages, and made sure oaths were kept. Thursday's energies influence relationships, weather magic (especially rain), and commitments.

FRIDAY   Friday was named after Frigg, whose name means "well beloved." In Teutonic tradition, Frigg was originally a moon goddess who also protected marriages. Friday continues to influence personal passions, devotion, love, and resourcefulness.

SATURDAY   Saturday was named after Saturn, a Roman vegetation god whose festivals included abundant feasting and socialization. Saturday's energies influence personal transitions, accent encouragement, and clarify the principle of reaping what we sow.

SUNDAY   As one might expect from the name, Sunday is the Sun's day. Since the Sun represents the god aspect and all its attributes, Sunday's energies influence logic, reasoning, leadership skills, and the conscious mind. It is also considered a "blessed day" for any solar-related magic.

Months and Associations

Month	Magical Energies	Chinese Calendar
January	Protection	Opportunity, prosperity
February	Healing, atonement	Conscious mind, kinship
March	Achievement, victory	Introspection, self
April	Luck, openings	Happiness, certainty
May	Progress, Earth magic	Health, strength
June	Love, devotion	Romance, luck, wit
July	Leadership, control	Joy, sensibility
August	Balance, harmony	Creativity, flexibility
September	Psychism, spirituality	Communication, artistry
October	Transitions (self)	Bravery, self-assurance
November	Compassion, patience	Devotion, service
December	Insight, wisdom	Virtue, the will, faith

Day Points

Time	Associations
Dawn	Beginnings, hope, the season of spring
Morning	Conscious mind, authority, keen perception
Noon	Sun magic, Fire magic, reason, banishing darkness, the season of summer
Dusk	Completion, closure, endings, the season of fall
Night	Rest, health, moon and star magic, the season of winter
Midnight	The witching hour: spirit communication, astral travel, fairy magic, glamoury

Moon Signs

Sign-Phase	Association
Dark moon	Rest, weeding out negativity, waiting
Waxing moon	Slow, steady growth
Full moon	Maturity, experience, lunar fullness
Waning moon	Banishing, decrease
Blue moon	Miracles

Sign-Phase	Association
In Pisces	Water magic, fertility, creativity
In Aquarius	Air element, motivation, communication
In Capricorn	Earth magic, development, foundations
In Sagittarius	Self mastery, prudence, attainment
In Scorpio	Fire magic, passion, investigation
In Libra	Symmetry, balance, fairness
In Virgo	Prosperity, success
In Leo	Sun magic, vitality, skill, courage
In Cancer	Moon magic, abundance, inventiveness
In Gemini	Harmony from diversity, transitions
In Taurus	Tenacity, steadfastness, resourcefulness
In Aries	Purification, artistry, overcoming barriers

Just for Fun: On what day of the week and in what month were you born? Compare the associations given for that day and month to your personality and traits. How have the energies affected you, if at all?

To put all this into a functional illustration, say you wanted to develop a personal art like writing or painting. A ritual or spell to help with this might best be planned for a Wednesday at dawn when the Moon is in Aries. Alternatively, you might use the same weekday and moon sign, but perform the ritual beneath a waxing or full moon to emphasize development. *Hint:* Copy this information into the section for creativity spells, or those for personal growth and improvement.

Effective Ritual Constructs

Every ritual will be slightly different in form, function, and outcome. Even so, there is a basic design that you can use any time you're preparing for, or creating, a ritual. I highly recommend keeping notes about this design, and any modifications you make, in your Book of Shadows since it's adaptable to any occasion.

Step One: An Outline

If you're working with a ritual written by someone else, you need to read it over and see if everything makes sense. Should there be problems with wording, actions, or tools, this is the time to make personally meaningful changes.

If you're creating a ritual from scratch, it never hurts to look over a few rituals designed for similar goals before making your own outline. The outline needs to include an opening for the ritual, the desired invocation, main activities, and a closing of some kind. A copy of this should be provided to anyone directly involved in casting the circle or directing the gathering so they can familiarize themselves with the outline beforehand.

Step Two: Finding a Location

This may or may not be a consideration (many people hold rituals right at home). *But,* if your ritual requires an outdoor setting, finding the right spot can take time and might even require a permit. Also, the accessories you choose in Step Three will be influenced by your location. Huge braziers might be fine outdoors, but not in an apartment, for example.

Step Three: Gathering Accessories

Your outline will determine what accessories you need for a ritual. If, for example, the invocation calls for lighting candles at the four Quarters, you will need four elementally-colored candles along with any other tools, costumes, aromatics, libations, etc. that the ritual calls for. *Note:* You might want to make a checklist of accessories so you don't forget a key item.

Please consider your space constraints and any allergies that your participants might have when making your accessory choices. Heavy incense can be stifling in small spaces, and sneezing throughout a ritual is not an effective release of power!

Reminder: Always cleanse and bless your ritual components before taking them into the sacred space. You want clean tools through which magical energy can flow unhindered.

Step Four: Preparing Your Space

Thoughtful set up is very important, especially outdoors where people can easily trip over greenery, loose twigs, and stones. Make sure each prop for the ritual is near the area where it needs to be used. Lay out the altar and Quarter points. Decorate the perimeter of the circle, if desired. Make sure any fire sources are safely away from curtains and other flammable objects.

Step Five: Open the Circle

The opening of a ritual includes the invocation (to create sacred space) and other techniques, like unified breathing, that help put the participants in the right frame of mind. Whatever your design, make sure that it somehow marks the line between temporal and spiritual thought and action. Find ways to leave the concrete world behind and focus wholly on the magical world within the circle.

Step Six: Building Energy

Each ritual is designed to build energy for a specific purpose. This can be accomplished through dancing, chanting, focused wills, guided meditation, and other central activities. Remember that "building" implies a progression. Central activities should be planned to raise energy in natural steps, both in the participants and in the sacred space. Rushing this process makes for very messy magic.

Step Seven: Releasing and Guiding the Magic

It amazes me how many times people forget to release power and guide it toward the goal (most often in spells, but it happens in ritual too). Here you have this wonderful cone of power "all dressed up with no place to go"! Think of releasing your magic similarly to letting go of a finely aimed arrow. Even though you know you've directed the arrow to the best of your ability, you still watch expectantly to see it land. Magic works like this too; your focus and hope help guide it where it needs to go. *Hint:* Cross-reference the above in the spell section of your book.

Step Eight: Closing

After all the buildup, the closing reconnects people with "terra firma," gives thanks to the Powers for their presence, and provides some sense of completion for the participants. Commonly the Quarters are dismissed as part of the closing, often accompanied by a final prayer or blessing.

Step Nine: Grounding and Integration

This is perhaps the most important part of any ritual. Since working magic can leave you a little light-headed, grounding gets your head out of the clouds. Two great ways of grounding are to simply sit on the earth for a while, letting your senses readjust, and eating raw vegetables. I find the crunch of the vegetables really brings me back into my body. *Hint:* You might want to add this information to the food section of your spellbook.

Here is a typical sample ritual to give you insight on how all the steps are incorporated:

Fall Ritual

The major Wiccan fall ritual takes place on or around September 21, the autumn equinox. This rite commemorates the harvest and the earth's generous gifts to us. Other themes for the observance include conservation, frugality, and sharing.

To prepare, gather apples, nuts, squash, pumpkins, grapes, and other freshly harvested edibles to decorate the circle. Use an orange-colored altar cloth littered with fall leaves and any candles you desire. Put a cup of grape wine or cider on the altar along with a Spirit candle, a handful of nuts, and a piece of black construction paper.

Invocation

This begins in the west, the region associated with fall metaphysically. Start this ritual at sunset, and if possible place at the four Quarters symbolic items that you can pick up and hold during the invocation (like a cup of water or a shell, seeds or soil, a fan, and a candle or incense).

WEST   *Lady of the Waters*
       I/we welcome your abundant energy
       Let my/our heart(s) overflow with gladness

NORTH *Earth mother*
       I/we welcome your harvest
       Let me/us reap seeds of character

EAST   *Lord of the Winds*
       I/we welcome your changes
       Let me/us breathe deeply the air of thoughtfulness

SOUTH *Fire Father*
       I/we welcome your warm protection
       Let me/us burn with Spirit's embers

The Ritual

Go to the altar and hold the cup high to the sky saying,

Gods and Goddesses of Earth and the harvest, you have been generous once more and now I/we return your kindness with thankful hearts.

Pour half the water in the cup onto the earth to return the gift given by the soil. (If you wish, you can put a fruit or vegetable seedling in the ground here too.) Pass the cup to all participants one at a time saying,

What is it you wish to harvest?

Each participant replies,

> *I harvest and accept the ability to*————. [Fill in the blank with
> the characteristic or attribute desired, and take a sip.]

If you're working the ritual alone, simply skip the "what is your
wish . . ." step. Replace the cup on the altar.

Afterward take the candle from the altar and hold it in both
hands while thinking intently about one question that lies heavy
on your heart. (Fall is a favored time for divinatory efforts.) Visualize the question in symbolic or literal terms, if possible. When
you feel ready, tip the candle toward the black paper so the wax
freely drips down saying,

> *Spirit of insight, reveal the answer.*
> *Open my inner sight so I can see what you place here.*

Let the candle keep dripping in a random pattern for three to four
minutes, then replace the candle. Let the paper dry through the
rest of the ritual; you can scry it for interpretive value later during
the grounding time.

Finally, hold both hands, palms down, over the nuts (shells on)
saying,

> *Spirit of Providence, Fill . . . Fill!*
> *By your power, by my will!*

Each participant should take one of the nuts home and open it
only when they have a pressing need. Opening the nut releases the
magic. At least one of these should be planted in the earth, too, to
fulfill the planet's needs.

Closing the Circle

Move counterclockwise, beginning in the East.

EAST   *The winds grow quiet, but the magic stays*
        to keep us/me judicious and thrifty each day.
        Hail and farewell.

NORTH   *The earth is weary, but potential remains*
            to grant strong foundations, when the sun wanes.
            Hail and Farewell.

WEST   *The waters chill, but house life deep within*
            to feed the spirit, so let the Wheel spin!
            Hail and Farewell.

SOUTH   *The fires die down, but the coals still burn*
            to maintain our soul, and the lessons it has learned.
            Hail and Farewell.

As for integration, if you worked the ritual with others talk about it! What seemed to flow the best? What parts did they like most? What's the overall consensus about success or failure? Use this feedback in designing future rituals. If you worked the ritual alone, all the same questions exist, so take the time to think over what just happened. For future reference, you might want to write your observations in the personal diary section of your Book of Shadows.

Hint for Success: Remember that your outline is only that, a guide. Listen closely to Spirit's leadings and your own intuitive instincts throughout the course of a ritual, and the outcome will always be more satisfying.

Seasonal and Lunar Rituals

Many Wiccan rituals focus on the Wheel of the Year: the passing of the seasons (the height of the sun in the sky) and the Moon's phases. Lunar rituals are called Esbats. Seasonal rituals are called Sabbats, Quarter festivals, or cross-quarter days. *Hint:* Add these definitions to your glossary.

The four main Sabbats are the spring equinox, summer solstice, fall equinox, and winter solstice. These four points equate to east-Air, south-Fire, west-Water, and north-Earth in the magic circle respectively, and they're the major points around which the Wheel of the Year revolves. *Hint:* You might want to add these correspondences to your elemental list. Between these festivals cross-quarter observances take place: Beltane, Lammas, Samhain, and Candlemas. Cross-quarter observances are held when fairy folk are said to come out of hiding! These are the eight festivals that *most* Wiccans observe regularly.

For future reference, add this chart or an adaptation of it to your Book of Shadows. Note that what I've provided here is a generalization combined with my own personal approaches. You'll probably want to expand upon this, adding history, folklore, the ways your tradition celebrates each event, and other similar information in the observance section of your Book of Shadows. So, leave extra room in the associated pages.

Festival and Date	*Magical Themes*
Beltane (5/1)	Fertility, rebirth, male-female energies, fate, luck, fairy kinship. Colors: spring green, raindrop blue, yellow, pink. Element: Air and Fire (earthy undertones). Symbols: braided ribbons, the maypole.
Summer solstice (6/21)	Fire, energy, socialization, vitality, relationship magic, magical herbalism. Element: Fire. Colors: red, gold, white-blue. Symbols: the tribal fire (any light source), fruits and flowers. Suggested aromatic: cinnamon.
Lammas (8/1)	Providence, the harvest, offerings of first fruits, fairy kinship. Element: Fire and Water Colors: bread-brown, grain-yellow, harvest tones. Symbols: sheaf of wheat, bread loaf, any first-harvested item.
Fall equinox (9/21)	Symmetry and balance, wise use of resources, harvest celebrations, fertility of earth. Element: Water. Colors: brown-red, orange, brown-yellow. Symbols: cornucopia, all harvest vegetables and fruits. Suggested aromatic: apple.
Samhain (11/1)	Death and rebirth, the new year, spirits interacting with humans, divination, magic. Element: Water and Earth. Colors: black, grey, vibrant red-orange (for protection). Symbols: carved pumpkin or turnip, witch animals, broomstick.

Festival and Date	Magical Themes
Winter solstice (12/21)	Commencement, hope, good fortune, kinship, tradition, the re-born sun. Element: Earth (fire undertones). Colors: brown, white, and evergreen. Symbols: the Yule tree (which represents offerings to nature spirits), mistletoe, holly. Suggested aromatic: pine.
Candlemas (2/2)	Health, omen observation, animal kinship, safety, improving finances. Element: Fire and Air (earth undertone). Color: white or silver. Symbol: a lit candle.
Spring equinox (3/21)	Rebirth, refreshment, joy, balance, freedom. Element: Air. Colors: pastels especially pale yellows and oranges like a rising sun. Symbols: new sprouts, early blossoming flowers, eggs. Suggested aromatic: cherry blossom.

Note: The colors for the seasons vary from traditional elemental colors because they derive from nature's language.

FUN PROJECT

Make an illustrated Wheel of the Year for your Book of Shadows. Start with a full page on which you draw a circle containing eight spokes radiating from the center. In each slice of the circle, put the name of the festival, some of its attributes and correspondences, and emblems that stress that theme. If you wish, add color to the slices and aromatic oils to accent the symbolism further.

Many practitioners also hold regular observances to honor the Moon's waxing and waning. While the exact purpose of each lunar festival will vary according to group, individual, and need, here's a general overview:

Dark moon rituals focus on reflection and introspection. This is a hushed moment just before everything begins anew, so we gather strength and prepare the soil of our soul. There need be no words in this ritual, only silence to honor the moment.

Waxing moon rituals focus on beginnings, steady growth, and awakening one's psychic self. The first glimpse of a waxing moon renews hope, and inspires our ability to dream. This represents the youthful goddess.

Full moon rituals focus on fertility, creativity, maturity, bearing fruit, and power. Here we can begin internalizing the mature Goddess and seeing Her within ourselves.

Waning moon rituals focus on banishing, diminishing, and cleansing negativity. As the Moon shrinks back to darkness, we get rid of personal shadows—outmoded ideas and ways of thinking—as the prelude to a new cycle. This represents the ancient crone goddess, full of wisdom.

Hint: You may wish to transfer or cross-reference these lunar correspondences for the goddess into the appropriate section of your spellbook.

Personal Rituals

As the Wheel of Life turns, other occasions arise when we want to call upon the Sacred powers. Perhaps they are to commemorate a birthday, to perform a blessing, to welcome a child, to mourn, to acknowledge an important historical event, or to give thanks. Whatever the reason, the Wiccan Wheel allows for, and encourages, such observances as a way of maintaining our connection with Spirit.

Personal rituals are a little different than those that honor seasons or other Wiccan observances because, well, they're personal! These rituals have similar constructs, but the way everything goes together depends a lot on the individual involved. For example, my morning ritual involves lighting a candle on my altar and saying good morning to the Goddess. It's short, sweet, to the point, and gets my day started on a positive keynote (i.e., welcoming the Sacred). From this one illustration, you can see that personal rituals don't have to be as involved as other traditional festivals, and they certainly don't have to be lengthy.

One well-considered, routinely repeated, personally meaningful ritual (be it five minutes or fifty) has the power to change your life. And, as with your other successful rituals, you'll want to make notes of the personal rituals you really like and find most useful in your Book of Shadows. Trust me when I say they'll come in handy over and over again not only for yourself, but for your magical friends as well.

Effectively enacting both seasonal and personal rituals regularly throughout the year creates a continuity of tradition. This gives our faith an outward shape that we can see and touch, and dance and sing to. These forms of expression also help us internalize the meaning of our faith as individuals and as a tribe, and fill our lives with the ebb and flow of magic.

Suggested Reading

Seasons of the Sun. Patricia Telesco. York Beach, Maine: Samuel Weiser, 1996.

365 Goddesses. Patricia Telesco. San Francisco: HarperCollins, 1998.

Holidays, Festivals, and Celebrations of the World Dictionary. Helene Henderson, Sue Ellen Thompson, eds. Detroit, Mich.: Omnigraphics, 1997.

Personal Notes

7

Divination Tools and Methods

Probably as soon as our ancestors understood the concept of "tomorrow" they wished to know what the future held. Also, our forebears used divination to better understand their past and present, and to get alternative perspectives on everyday problems. We are certainly no different, which is why having a section on this subject in your Book of Shadows is so helpful.

One of the goals of practicing Wicca is to teach yourself to look beyond surface reality into the unseen realms. Divination tools and techniques offer us an effective way of doing that through a serviceable, often convenient, medium. By collecting a variety of divination techniques into your spellbook, you can find one (a) that makes sense considering your question and circumstances; (b) whose components you have available; and (c) that you also like to use.

The purpose of this chapter is fourfold. First, it provides instructions on how to prepare yourself for any divination effort. Second, it discusses several time-honored divination mediums that I personally enjoy using. Third, it furnishes some good dos and don'ts in regard to the way you read any divination system.

117

Fourth, it discusses the process for making your own divination system—one that's really meaningful to you and created from the ground up by your own hands. Take what you find most useful in each of these sections and transfer it into the appropriate section of your Book of Shadows.

Personal Preparation

Personal preparation is one half of the equation to achieving sensitive accuracy in your divination procedure. No matter how good a reader you may be, or how refined your divinatory system, if you're not ready the reading is going to suffer. The following prep routine is the one that I use. Read this over, tweak it, then copy it into your spellbook and use it regularly. Why? Because the more you follow the same procedure, the more it becomes a mini-ritual that puts you in the right spiritual mindset for everything to come.

Divination Prep Work

1. If possible, fast for a period of time beforehand. This helps with cleansing and turns your attention away from physical matters.
2. Take a relaxing herbal bath or shower beforehand. Again, this has a cleansing effect. It also relaxes you. Stress is a terrible deterrent to the flow of a good reading. If time doesn't allow this, simply wash your hands, focusing your negativity into them so you can rinse the psychic dirt down the drain.

   Note: No. 1 and no. 2 also work for pre-ritual self preparation.

3. Consider finding an aromatic (incense, oil, perfume, or whatever) that you can use to establish an auric ambiance conducive to psychic insight. I like frankincense and myrrh oil, which I rub lightly on my palms, temples, and third eye. Other good psychic aromas include: rose, mint, sandalwood, nutmeg, and lilac. *Hint:* You may want to copy these associations into the herbal section of your Book of Shadows.

4. Add yellow highlights into your work space to stress the psychic, creative, intuitive self. Also anything colored silver (lunar) stresses these attributes. *Hint:* Copy these correspondences into the color section of your spellbook.

5. If you find it helps you concentrate, pick out some instrumental music and play this piece each time you do a reading. Light bells, even-toned drumming, chimes, and the sound of waves combined with music all seem to help me connect with the intuitive nature. You'll probably have to experiment to discover which sounds work best for you. *Hint:* Music, especially drumming, is a tremendous helpmate to meditation and trance work, so you may want to cross-reference this point in that section of your Book of Shadows.

6. Set up the reading area so it's comfortable. Dimmed lighting helps, but make sure you can see your tools clearly and, if you're reading for someone else, the eyes of the querent. You'll also want to have note paper or a tape recorder handy so you can transcribe the reading. This way you can go back to it later for deeper insights and understanding.

7. Do everything in your power to shake off any personal notions of how you think the reading should progress. Preconceptions can change the energy in the tool, or change the way you read the outcome. If you ever feel you can't set aside "self"—either don't go forward with the reading, or ask someone else to do it.

   If you're reading for someone else, you can avoid this pitfall by telling them *not* to verbalize their question until after the reading. This approach keeps you from hunting for meanings that may or may not be there. If it's a reading you planned for yourself, I suggest getting a magical associate to perform the reading for you instead. This way you'll have more emotional distance.

8. If for any reason you get a bad feeling about a reading before your begin, stop right away. Pick up the tool, cleanse it of any random energies, shake off any vibrations that might be clinging to you, and try again. If it happens twice, don't try again today. Something's amiss and it's better to wait for more auspicious circumstances. *Hint:* Always trust your instincts before you enact any form of magic. If it doesn't feel right, and you

can't fix whatever seems off, don't ignore what Spirit and your inner voice are telling you.

Divination Mediums

The world's history is filled with literally hundreds, if not thousands, of different divination media. From dirt and dice to stones and stars, everything on or around humankind was assessed as having some value for predicting fate. This concept had its foundations in animistic belief systems that saw spirits in every creature, tree, element, etc. And while Wiccans may not always hold the same worldview as our ancestors, we still often use similar divination systems that originate in nature's storehouse. Thanks to the wonders of technology, we also have an abundance of new systems to consider.

Since it would be impossible to review all of these mediums in this book, what I'd like to do instead is give you some handy definitions for your Book of Shadows, some guidelines for choosing a system that's right for you and caring for it properly, and a glimpse into a few interesting mediums that you can easily try at home.

Defining Terms

Before we begin looking at any of the types of divination media that have been commonly used, it helps to understand some of the terminology associated with divination systems and readers. Here's a list of words to add to your spellbook's glossary:

Augury   Divination by the observation of birds, celestial events, random encounters with animals, and other sign observations. This was considered an occupation in ancient Rome.

Automatism   A divination method wherein a medium channels a spirit, who then subsequently writes or draws a message for the querent (as with automatic writing).

Binary Divination   Any divination system that offers a yes/no type answer.

Cast System   Any system that is mixed, and then cast upon a surface, and the subsequent patterns or the object's resting locations are then interpreted.

Drawn System   Like the Tarot: Any divination system where the querent draws out an item in response to a question.

Geomantic System   Any system that draws its interpretive values from the earth's configurations or patterns. Soil scattering, cloud scrying, Feng Shui, and similar systems are all geomantic.

Media   The basic components of the divination system. With the Tarot, for example, cards are the media. For a channeler, his or her own body becomes the media. Here we find the importance between "reading" an oracle, and "becoming" the oracle. Both methods can result in good readings; it's simply a matter of which approach suits you best.

Medium   A medium is a person who acts like an interdimensional phone line, carrying messages between the worlds. Sometimes a medium also allows a spirit to temporarily use his or her body to communicate.

Omen   Any casual event thought to predict something in the near future (such as a red sun at dusk indicating a potential storm for the next day).

Oracle   Inspired mediums who often work in the service of a specific deity, such as the Delphic Oracle in Greece, which represented Apollo.

Prophet   Someone who foretells events, often without the aid of omens, signs, or other tools. Prophets are frequently considered divinely inspired.

Querent   The person asking the question in a reading.

Random Divination   Divination methods that take their interpretive value from things that the querent cannot control, such as finding a penny (portends luck), etc. *Hint:* Pennies still make an excellent, handy component for luck magic. You might want to make note of this in the spell section of your Book of Shadows.

Reader The term reader refers to the person who will interpret the divination system being used for the person asking the question. When doing fortune telling for yourself, you become both the querent and the reader.

Scrying Divination systems that entail close observation of an object or item and any subsequent visions. The flame of a candle or a crystal ball are two examples of objects used for scrying. *Hint:* You may wish to add a crystal ball to the tool list in your Book of Shadows. You can obtain such crystals with polished surfaces at science shops and new age stores.

Second Sight Also called "the sight," people with this gift need no tools to predict the future, although, unlike the prophet, they're not regarded as necessary divinely inspired. Also, frequently this seer's ability is influenced by external stimulation, like touching a person or object. Psychics might be considered in this category.

Sign Signs are like omens, except that in some cases a diviner may do something to stimulate a sign. For example, a Greek diviner might have startled a flock of birds and watched their movements for a sign. *Hint:* You may wish to cross-reference this information with your spellbook's section on animal symbolism.

Okay, now that we know what's what, it's easier to begin considering various forms of divination. To my thinking these "forms" can really be subcategorized into two main types: divination systems whose media originate in nature, and those whose media have been contrived by human minds and hands.

Natural Media

By the above definition, these divination systems have media or interpretive values that originate in nature's classroom. In considering the state of the earth, preserving and using these forms of divination is very important because it keeps us connected with Gaia, her cycles, and her voice.

In this category we find methods like interpreting the meaning in found feathers, the omens and signs provided by animals, observation of celestial objects and events (like astrology), casting stones, watching plant growth, noting the position of a rainbow, listening to the wind or thunder, and the like. In fact, I would hazard a guess that there's likely nothing on, or above, this planet that hasn't been used for fortune-telling at least once!

Sometimes a diviner who works with natural media adds something to the base to create a slightly different tool. For example, rather than watching plant growth a diviner might burn a dried herb and observe its smoke. Or, rather than wait for a moving water source to "speak" the omen an interpreter might toss in a pebble and observe the ripples. These minor changes allow for more immediate responses.

The only difficulty in using all natural media for divination, especially for the city dweller, is the availability of materials. These days one doesn't often see an animal (say a fox) by happenstance because there are few truly wild regions left near where we live. So we're left to adapt these systems to the human condition. For example, rather than watching for a natural creature to cross your path, perhaps you can watch for animals in commercials, logos, bumper stickers, etc.

Fabricated Media

In adapting traditional interpretations for natural media to our modern world, we come across fabricated media offering yet more options. Included in this category are Tarot decks, pendulum kits, rune sets, Ouija boards, angel cards, mah-jongg tiles, dice, the luck ball, wax drippings on water, bibliomancy, tea leaf reading, dowsing, palmistry, and domino divination, just to name a few. This amazingly diversified list indicates that humankind has wasted no ingenuity in its attempts to find effective fortune-telling tools! The hard part for us comes in choosing among them all.

Choosing a System

In choosing one or several divination systems that you'll use regularly, the interpretations for which you'll maintain in your Book of Shadows, and the results from which you'll keep in your Magical Diary, there are several things to consider. First, what sense do you respond to most strongly? You will want to choose at least one divination system that activates this primary sense.

For example, highly visual people will enjoy systems like the Tarot or other decks because these offer strong visual input. Tactile people will likely prefer stones, runes, or other objects that have textural appeal. People who are drawn to sound might try listening to the voice of the elements (wind, water, earth sounds, crackling fire), and those who are stimulated by aromas might burn aromatic herbs as a focus, then interpret the resulting smells (harsh, pleasant, fresh, musty, etc.) along with the smoke's movement.

Second, how do you think? Are you the logical sort, or more intuitive? Logical people will need concrete systems with a specific symbol equating to one or two interpretive values. Intuitive people can turn to ink blots, the patterns in castings, and other less right-brain methods.

Third, how detailed do you think your questions are going to be? Binary systems, like drawing lots, don't give you a lot of interpretive values other than variants of yes and no. For example, a pendulum moving up and down may indicate any of these very general positive responses: yes, go, good, move. Conversely, left to right movements are negative: no, stop, bad, halt. Mind you, if your question was more detailed in nature, this type of system won't work. So, I suggest having one or two binary systems featured in your Book of Shadows for general questions, and the specifics of at least one more detail-oriented system that can handle other complex or multifaceted questions.

Personalizing the System

Divination is no different from any other magical method: personal vision is a key component to success. So, if a divination system's interpretation guide says one thing, and your heart says another, listen to your heart. It's good to know the traditional associations to give those intuitive moments more dimension, but ultimately your inner voice must guide you on how to interpret any reading.

To give you an example that includes both traditional and personal correspondences for a divination system, here are a few runes as I've listed them in my own Book of Shadows. If you find this useful, feel free to copy it into yours (but I suggest adding a visual image of the rune, too, so you begin to associate the symbol with its meaning).

Rune	Traditional	Personal Variances
Mannaz	Growth and change	A doorway or choice
Isa	An impasse	The self (alone)
Othila	Separation	Pilgrimage
Algiz	Safety, protection	Security; Living presently
Teiwaz	Warrior self	Reaching aims courageously
Sowelu	Sun, wholeness	Flash of insight; act on it
Dagaz	Accomplishment	Creation, balance
Kano	Fire, light	Opportunity knocking

Care and Keeping of Your Tools

If you choose a divination tool like the Tarot, runes, or a crystal set, you'll want to take proper care of it. That means regular maintenance to keep the tool free of collected energies, specifically those it picks up during a reading. It also means keeping it safely stored between uses.

The same maintenance methods you noted for your personal magical tools can certainly be applied to divination sets. So, cross-reference that information in the divination part of your Book of Shadows. Additionally, any other techniques you find yourself using with a particular system should be noted here. For example, for my crystal casting set I have the following specific notes in the divination guide for this system:

- Cleanse the stones in a salt or lemon-water bath once a month.
- Keep them wrapped in a white linen cloth between uses.
- Aurically pull away any residual energies lingering on the stones between readings.
- Regularly visualize the stones being filled to overflowing with white, purifying light that replaces any darkness.
- Regularly charge the stone set in sunlight and moonlight to keep their energies balanced and at maximum capacity.
- Periodically carry the stones or sleep with them under a pillow to increase my sensitivity to their vibrations.

For more information about divination systems and methods, refer to my book *Fortune-telling: A Complete Guide to Divination* (Freedom, CA: Crossing Press, 1998).

Reading Dos and Don'ts

Beyond finding the right tools for you and the question at hand, and caring for your divination systems properly, there are other dos and don'ts that produce more positive results in readings. These are provided here for your reference. You may want to include them in your Book of Shadows under "Reading Guidelines, Helps, and Hints" or something similar.

1. Remember that the universe often tells us about things that we haven't asked about, but *need* to hear about. So, remain open to Spirit. Don't get stuck in concrete thinking. When these unexpected but timely responses come through your tools it's usually an important message.
2. No matter who you're reading for, remember that divination media should not give you threatening or vicious results. When this happens, something's wrong and you should stop the reading immediately. For example, the Ouija board can sometimes indicate the presence of a malicious spirit who doesn't have your best interests in mind.

3. Use positive, constructive words when interpreting a reading. There is almost always a good method for communicating bad news.

4. Referring to number 3, always remember, too, that life is what you or the querent choose to make of it. Even when a reading seems bad, your choices here and now can change everything.

5. If you do readings for others, regularly do a "self check" for ethics. For example, if you can't put aside negative feelings toward the querent, politely decline to do the reading. If you decide to accept trade or barter for your time, keep your requests reasonable and in keeping with the querent's ability to reciprocate. Remember, while people tend to appreciate what they pay for, a person's spiritual life shouldn't be limited by cash flow (or lack thereof).

6. Remember that not all readings are going to be "right on." There are many circumstances that can muddle a reading, not the least of which are noise and interruptions. When this happens, try again or pull some extra cards, stones, or whatever to clarify your results. If you still get a really confusing reading, make notes of it and review them later. Sometimes a reading's interpretation doesn't make sense until days or weeks later.

7. Don't let divination become a crutch. Use it when you need an alternative perspective, but remember no fortune-telling method can determine your future. Only you can do that.

Making Your Own Divination System

Just so you know, there's nothing that says you can't make your own divination system. Look at the ones you like to use, then come up with a media that works within that type of construct. Use symbols, colors, and components that have deep meaning to you. Make notes of the meanings for each item in your Book of Shadows, then enjoy the insight the tool gives you.

Personal Notes

_____
_____
_____
_____
_____
_____
_____
_____
_____
_____
_____
_____
_____
_____
_____

8

Elements, Correspondences, and Applications

It is nearly impossible to discuss magic without also talking about the elements, their meaning, and the way the energy of the elements gets applied in various mystical procedures. Elemental correspondences influence a great deal of magical work from choosing spell components to the way one invokes the Quarters in a circle. So, this section of your Book of Shadows is likely to see a lot of use!

I will give you as much foundational information here as possible, but please bear in mind that elemental correspondences vary slightly throughout magical traditions, and show even more variance in distinct cultural settings. So, what I'm providing for your spellbook is the "101" course. To these materials you will eventually want to add:

- How to recognize the presence of elemental beings. (Some examples of this are included in this section.)
- How to call and work with elemental beings. *Hint:* You may want to add elemental callings into the ritual portion of your spellbook to use as alternative invocations.

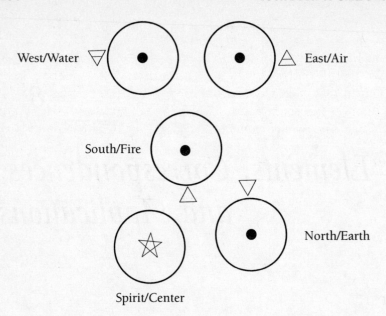

- How to create and empower elementaries. *Hint:* Add this defini-tion to your glossary. An elementary is a miniature elemental being that you create, empower, and give a specific task. This is considered an adept form of magic that shouldn't be undertaken without serious training.
- Elemental meditations and visualizations that help attune you to those energies. *Hint:* These meditations help with spellcraft and ritual work too, especially those aligned with one specific ele-ment that gives shape to the whole procedure.
- How to access the middle realm of the shamanic World Tree to learn more about the elements. *Hint:* If you begin this type of work, you may want to add a special section to your Book of Shadows on astral travel, its uses, and any successful methods you find for same.
- More complete elemental correspondences for animals, plants, stones, objects, etc. as you find them or intuitively discover them. *Hint:* Cross-reference these correspondences in the appro-priate sections of your spellbook.

The Internal Elemental Wheel

In chapter 6 of this book, I shared with you the correspondences for the seasons, which are part of the great cosmic Wheel. I mentioned that, generally speaking, spring and east equates with Air, summer and south equates with Fire, fall and west equates with Water, and winter and north equates with Earth. If you don't already have these associations on your seasonal Wheel, add or cross-reference them now.

The elemental Wheel is very important to understanding the overall worldview of Wiccans. The Wheel is ever in motion—along its path energy is never destroyed, and is forever changing shape, being recycled and reformed into something new. So as Air moves into Fire, the fire burns brighter. As Fire moves into Water, it dulls and the water warms. As Water moves into Earth, it fertilizes or freezes, and as Earth moves into Air, it's dispersed and the cycle is fulfilled. In this manner, no element stands alone—it is equal on the circle and touches all the other elements at the center point, which is Spirit.

So, the elements are part of everything that we are substantively and spiritually. To better understand this connection, here's a chart that shows how the elements portray your life's cycle. *Hint:* add this information to your elemental correspondence lists:

Air	*Fire*	*Water*	*Earth*
Birth	Child	Adult	Elder
Waking	Active	Fulfilled	Rest
Knowledge	Will	Courage	Silence

At birth the child comes forth from the womb, grasps its first breath of air, and awakens to a whole new world. This is the dawn of life. Every moment of existence at this point now becomes a learning experience, our hungry minds ever reaching for more understanding.

As a young child, we are full of energy, experiencing each day completely. At this point we are the center of our universe, totally willful and believing that our desires deserve attention. These characteristics represent the active principle of Fire.

Slowly, the Fire's energy calms into a new maturity and awareness. We learn to flow with life; we learn there is a time to weep, a time to love, to stand our ground, and a time to rejoice. This is the emotional influence of Water. Finally we reach our elder years, where like a great oak we have reached as far as we can. The wisdom within knows when to speak and when to remain silent. We also recognize that a new cycle lies just around the corner. This is the rooted, calm nature of Earth expressing itself, the Earth to which our bodies will return as our spirits take flight back to Air.

As you begin to understand the elements in your life and body, a natural curiosity arises about how they evidence themselves in everything else. Exactly how something got categorized as one element versus another is actually more obvious than you might think. Hot herbs like garlic, for example, were Fire. White and round vegetables like cabbage were associated with Water because of their connection with the Moon.

So our ancestors looked to the color, aroma, flavor, texture, shape, and known uses for a plant, stone, or whatever, to identify its elemental association. These sensual cues are something you can readily use in guessing something's elemental correspondence if you don't have it handy in your spellbook. For example, something that's brown or green in color, and has a coarse texture, is likely associated strongly with Earth. The lists that follow in this chapter will help you increase your understanding of the elements.

Air

The Air element is the first point of calling in almost all sacred circles. Here we stand at the edge of beginning, poised between darkness and dawn, sounds and silences. As the first rays of light touch the horizon everything around us awakens—the sounds are vibrant and welcoming. The winds are fresh and motivating. They fill our lungs with a cool warmth, the comfort of another day in which to grow and learn.

On a personal level the Air element represents our need to keep moving and learning. The human quest for knowledge and our curiosity are both outward manifestations of Air energies. Air also illustrates how one can affect his or her surroundings without being conspicuous—wind moves the leaves but we don't see it, we only see what it affects. Meditate on this idea and make notes in your Magical Diary about your insights.

AIR CORRESPONDENCES

Animals Birds
Astrological Signs Libra, Gemini, Aquarius
Chakara Throat
Color Pale yellow, pastels
Gift Truth sense, clairaudience
Emotions Cheer, hopefulness, a sense of freedom
Key words Communication, movement, the mind, beginnings
Moon Waxing crescent
Musical Expression Singing, chanting, mantras, toning
Physical Expression Breathing, language
Plants Dandelion, bluebell
Season Spring
Sense Hearing
Shape Octahedron or a circle with a dot in the center
Sounds Bells, wind chimes
Stones Aventurine, pumice
Spirit The playful sylphs, who look like the winged fairies of folklore
Time Dawn
Tool Wand, aromatic

Hint: When copying the correspondences you want into your spellbook, you may want to add more subcategories like herbs, planets, aromatics, winds, Cabalistic (or other cultural) variants, gods and goddesses, etc.

Fire

Turning clockwise around the circle, following the natural movement of the Sun, we arrive at the south and the element of Fire. The brightness of this light banishes the shadows. Here there is no dark-ness—only crackling fullness, passion, and the zest of being wholly participatory in the moment. The sun dances high in the sky, and with it our hearts beat, our feet dance, we live, and we love.

FIRE CORRESPONDENCES

Animals   Komodo dragon, desert-dwelling animals, lion
Astrological Signs   Aries, Leo, Sagittarius
Chakara   Heart
Color   Red, orange, gold
Gift   Illumination, attentiveness, purification
Emotion   Yearning, passion, will, energy
Key Words   Growth, activity, vitality
Moon   Full
Musical Expression   Drumming
Physical Expression   Heartbeat, body heat
Plants   Basil, fennel, onion
Season   Summer
Sense   Sight
Shape   Tetrahedron, triangle (point up)
Sounds   Static, crackling
Spirit   The joyful, exuberant Salamander
Stones   Amber, ruby, carnelian, garnet, lava
Time   Noon
Tool   Athame

The Fire element represents our energetic nature, the fires of body and soul. By studying Fire we learn how to use our energy effectively, how to feed and tend our internal flame without "burning out."

Water

As the circle turns once again, we find ourselves at the western quarter in the element of Water. Here the Earth's tears rain down to fertilize the soil. Our emotions grow into fullness of expression and we rediscover our psychic, spiritual selves. Water is stronger than it appears, quelling the fires that threaten to burn out of control. Yet it ebbs and wanes gently, following the Moon, and honing our soul.

WATER CORRESPONDENCES

Animals   Fish, seals, walrus

Astrological Signs   Cancer, Pisces, Scorpio

Chakara   Sacral plexus

Color   Blue, aquamarine, bluish-silver

Gift   Inventiveness, imagination, fertility

Emotion   Compassion, accomplishment, courage

Key Words   Harvest, flow, superconscious mind

Moon   Waning crescent

Musical Expression   Prayer bowls, gong

Physical Expression   Tears, saliva, perspiration

Plants   Willow, lettuce, kelp

Season   Autumn

Sense   Taste

Shape   Eicosahedron, trident

Sounds   Raindrops, waves

Spirit   Undine

Stones   Moonstone, silver, pearl

Time   Dusk

Tool   Cup

The most obvious lessons of the Water element are twofold. First we can learn to flow intuitively with life, with the energies of the universe, so that our reality smoothes out. Second, this fluid nature doesn't impede our capacity to be strong and stand our ground when need be. Water is patient, knowing that it takes time to wear away rock, but that, with persistence, the rock will give way. The same holds true for those proverbial brick walls in our lives—be as tenacious and patient as the water, and eventually you'll find a way to flow through!

Earth

Upon completing the outer circle, the final destination is Earth at the northern point. This is the Mother Spirit in whom we are rooted. Here the seeds of our being are sustained, fed, and nurtured

EARTH CORRESPONDENCES

Animals   Cow, snake, stag
Astrological Signs   Taurus, Virgo, Capricorn
Chakara   Root
Color   Brown, black, green
Gift   Faith
Emotion   Confidence, determination
Key Words   Money, structure, nature, support
Moon   Dark
Musical Expression   Brass instruments (other metalics)
Physical Expression   Sense of balance, tactile responses
Plants   Ivy, oats, corn, rice, oak
Season   Winter
Sense   Touch
Shape   Cube, circle with equidistant cross as radius
Sounds   Echos
Spirit   The tenacious, hard-working gnome
Stones   Green agate, coal, salt, turquoise
Time   Night
Tool   Coin, pentacle

into maturity. This sustenance is not without some materiality, for our body lives in a very real world with very real needs. Consequently the Earth element's lesson is one of sensibility, practicality, and wisdom. It teaches us that while we reach for the stars, our feet still stand on terra firma, and it's a good place to be! It also shows us that the deeper we put down roots, the greater capacity we have to reach up to heaven without toppling from overextension.

Spirit

Many mystical traditions add a fifth element, designated as Ether, the Void, or simply Spirit. This element is effectively the "duct

---

SPIRIT CORRESPONDENCES

Animals   Mythical creatures, white buffalo

Astrological Signs   The entire zodiac

Chakara   Crown, third eye

Color   Silver, white, rainbow

Gift   Unity, wholeness

Emotion   Selflessness, mercy

Key Words   Transform, transcend, self-awareness, internalize, express

Moon   Blue

Musical Expression   The orchestra or chorus

Physical Expression   Brain waves

Plants   Ephedra, mistletoe, the World Tree

Season   The Wheel in motion

Sense   Spiritual senses (hearing the inner voice)

Shape   DNA, dodecahedron

Sounds   Silence

Spirit   God/dess

Stones   Fossils, petrified wood

Time   Out of space, out of time

Tool   Self, cauldron

tape" for all the others—it binds, unites, harmonizes, and directs them as effectively as a talented conductor guides an orchestra. In the sacred circle, the location for the fifth element is twofold: the center, and the entire sphere (in other words, it is both within and without). While most priests and priestesses will stand in the center to invoke this energy, they do so realizing that such immenseness cannot be limited to the designated sacred space.

The fifth element represents the unknowable things in the universe—those things that go beyond surface reality, beyond space and time. It also symbolizes our ability to transcend the human frame, and the capacity of our spirits to reach out and touch the eternal. In this manner, the Spirit element embodies enlightenment and empowers us in our efforts to reunite with the Source.

Elemental Magic

Having all these charts neatly in hand and keeping them updated in your Book of Shadows doesn't necessarily help with the mechanical end of things. Right now you have raw data. This section will give you ideas on how to apply that data effectively for any magical effort.

Element	Magical Themes
Air	Movement, messages, knowledge (the mind)
Fire	Energy, relationships, physicality (the body), solar magic
Water	Healing, intuition, feelings (the emotions), lunar magic
Earth	Grounding, stability, finances (our roots)
Spirit	Unity, harmony, enlightenment, peace (the soul)

So, in spellcraft, when the theme of your spell corresponds with a specific element, you should accent that element somehow throughout the procedure. You can do this by:

• Choosing your components according to their elemental associations. For example, a spell for physical energy might include

ginger tea (ginger is Fire and the tea is heated, also symboliz-
ing Fire).
- Working with that specific element as a focal or prop. A healing
  spell, for example, might use flowing water as a reinforcement
  that washes away sickness.
- Using the element to help bear the magic. Communication
  spells, for example, might be sung into a suitable wind (a
  southerly wind to communicate to a loved one, a westerly wind
  to communicate your feelings effectively, an easterly wind for a
  fresh start in discourse, and a northerly wind for conversations
  focused on concrete matters). *Hint:* Copy the above spell ideas
  into the spellcraft section of your book. Also copy the wind correspondences into your elemental tables.

These same concepts translate well into meditation and trance
work. In this case, when the theme of a meditation or the purpose
of a trance has strong elemental overtones, surrounding yourself
with symbols of that element will help tremendously. For example,
if you're trying to get more grounded, you could meditate on the
image of a tree (for roots) and surround yourself with earthy
smells. Sitting on the ground to connect with Earth during the
meditation would be effective, as would putting your fingers in a
pot of rich soil. Going one step further, you could wait to try this
meditation until the Moon is dark. Also consider wearing brown
clothing, holding a green agate, and listening to nature sounds on
a compact disc or tape to further emphasize the Earth element.
Hint: Copy these ideas into the meditation section of your Book of
Shadows, and come up with other similar ideas for the remaining
three to four elements (depending on the system you prefer).

Finally, the elements are also obviously applied in the magic circle by calling the Quarters. Beyond this, however, there are other
ways to bring the elemental powers actively into a ritual. For
example, during an Earth Day ritual you might want to have everyone bring seeds or seedlings into the sacred space as a way of honoring Earth. Later those energized seeds will be planted to help
re-green the planet, and they might even have an earth-elemental

spirit attached to them thanks to your efforts. This particular ritual might be held inside a sacred square (rather than a circle) to stress the Earth element, and it could be marked with coins, grains, and other "earthy" substances. In this manner, everything in and around the sacred space calls to the Earth, who may then send an emissary to help you with the magic created. *Hint:* Copy the above ideas into the ritual portion of your spellbook.

Suggested Reading

The Wisdom of the Elements. Margie McArthur. Freedom, Calif.: Crossing Press, 1998.
Dancing With Devas. Tricia Telesco. New York: Toad Hall, 1999.
The Four Fold Way. Angeles Arrien. San Francisco: HarperCollins, 1993.

Personal Notes

9

Food and Beverage Correspondences and Applications

As an ardent "kitchen witch," this is by far the largest section in my personal Book of Shadows. I absolutely love cooking magic. I figure that I have to eat anyway, so why not make a potent ritual out of the whole procedure? If you follow my lead and copy the hints in this chapter into your spellbook, what you'll have at the end is something that feeds both body and spirit from one hearty platter!

The Magical Pantry's Tools and Techniques

Early in this book I talked about updating the tool list you keep in your Book of Shadows to include magical uses for everyday items. The kitchen provides an abundance of potential tools for "whipping up magic" if you look around with a truly creative and insightful eye. For example, I use my blender in beverages that I'm making for continuity (or for any food where I want to really "blend" energy), and my onion chopper in magical foods aimed at cutting up tension! But really these two examples are but the tip of the proverbial iceberg. *Hint:* Add these last two ideas to your tool list.

EXERCISE

Over one week's time, look through all your kitchen and pantry cupboards. Make a list of everything there (including canned goods, spices, utensils, etc.). Then, as you think of magical associations or corollaries between that item and a traditional tool, note it (don't overlook brand names and logos as sources for ideas). Copy these into your Book of Shadows.

In doing this exercise myself, I was very surprised at how many things I could use for (or adapt to) kitchen magic, all of which are very meaningful to me because I already use them nearly every day. Here's an abbreviated list of these items from my spellbook. If you find they make sense to you, add them to those from your own list in this section of your Book of Shadows.

KITCHEN AND PANTRY ACCESSORY ASSOCIATIONS

Hint: You'll probably want to copy or cross-reference some of these listings with the elemental, spellcraft, and tools section of your Book of Shadows.

Broom and dustpan   yin/yang energy in balance
Butter or steak knife   athame

Cookbook   your Book of Shadows (of course!)

Cutting board (or countertop)   the altar

Disposal or compost box   Earth element

Exhaust fan, open window, air conditioner   Air element

Fork   penetrating the surface to reveal truth

Freezer   halting negativity; cooling anger; preserving magical energy for a later date *Hint:* Mark your freezer bags with the theme of the food so you can warm up that energy any time!

Measuring cup   cup

Mixing bowl   goddess image

Pot   cauldron

Rolling pin   even temperedness, forbearance, control (also alternative wand or god image)

Sink   Water element

Spoon (wooden)   wand

Storage containers   protective, sustaining energy

Stove or microwave   Fire element

Thermometer   carefully monitoring one's emotions or a situation

Timer   timing the magic so it bakes up just right (the sounding of a bell helps with manifestation, especially if you include it in your incantation)

Turkey baster   god image

Now that you have some good ideas about the symbolic value of items that will soon become your magical tools, the next thing to consider is your methodology. Cooking, by nature, is very ritualistic, so it won't take much extra effort to turn your kitchen into a sacred space. Call the Quarters while you gather ingredients, choosing these carefully for their magical associations. Light a candle near your stove to represent the hearth god/dess, and bless the components while you're mixing, chopping, or whatever. *Hint:* Cross-reference this use for candles in the tool list. Keep a strong image of your goal in mind while you work, and let that intention saturate every part of the meal you're preparing.

In reviewing cooking magic around the world (and trust me when I say there's a lot of it), I found many methods were used to energize everything from single items to whole menus. In addition to this foundation, I've come up with a few approaches myself. Look these over and see which ones are most suited to your pantry's sacred space, then add those to your Book of Shadows:

• For any foods and beverages that rise or age, prepare them during a waxing to full moon to help this process go smoothly.

• For health, happiness, and general well-being, always stir mixtures clockwise to encourage positive energy. This is also said to help bread to rise, and beer to ferment properly.

• Whenever possible, put together your recipe's ingredients in an order that helps the manifesting energy progress naturally. (Ideas along these lines should already be in the spellcraft portion of your Book of Shadows—refer to chapter 4.)

• When creating recipes or menus from scratch, don't forget that the number of ingredients or their color can be used for magical symbolism. For example, a love potion might use two basic ingredients to represent partnership, while a meal for grounding might be prepared from four foods with predominantly brown or green coloring. *Hint:* Copy these associations into the color-numerical section of your spellbook. Refer to chapter 11 for more ideas along these lines.

> *Point of Interest:* The use of color and number symbolism appears regularly in magical herbalism, especially that of the Middle Ages. Since many of these herbal preparations were made at home, caring for the health and welfare of your loved ones is a celebrated custom that kitchen witches can reclaim!

• Don't forget your favorite ritual accents: work during an auspicious astrological phase, play music, burn some incense, chant, pray, or sing while you work, decorate your kitchen with magical embellishments, and the like. Do whatever it takes to transform mundane meals into magical masterpieces.

• Whenever you're preparing foods or beverages aimed at love and kinship, keep a candle burning nearby (or a light) for as long as possible. This comes from the old tradition in which the hearth fire represents emotional warmth in the home.

• Fairy folk *love* kitchen magic. If you'd like to invite their presence leave out a little gift of sweet cream or honey bread near the stove. *Hint:* Cross-reference this information under "elemental beings" in your spellbook.

• If performing pantry enchantments in any kitchen other than your own, always ask permission of the owner first. Not to do so insults the hearth guardians, and the magic won't work.

• In cooking magic, more does not equal better. Even one purposefully chosen and blessed ingredient can change a recipe's whole vibration. Just make sure your choices are tasty. (Food magic doesn't work very well if you can't eat the results!)

• Always refer to familial lore in considering your culinary wizardry. If a food or beverage has specific meaning to you because of (a) when it was prepared, (b) why it was prepared, or (c) an oral legacy, use that association over any found in books.

> *Important Note:* This kind of personalization applies to all magical methods, not just kitchen magic. In the end, customizing your methods generates meaningfulness and more powerful manifestations.

Nectar of the Gods (and Goddesses)

A lot of people don't realize that some of the first offerings considered suitable to the god/dess were those of clear water, milk, and alcoholic beverages. Why? Because the water and milk sustained life, and the "whys" of alcohol production were still a mystery, so people attributed the wonder to the divine. In fact, many beverages became strongly associated with specific god/desses, like Bragi (Norse—mead), Ceres (Roman—beer), Dionysus (Greek—wine), and Isis (Egypt—milk). *Hint:* Copy the above associations into the god and goddess portion of your Book of Shadows so you have available some appropriate offering ideas.

In making potent potions, you can consider the base ingredients for their magical associations. For example, peach juice might be quaffed for wisdom since peaches are noted as a sagacious fruit. To this base you might add a dollop of honey to stress that goal. Similarly, passion fruit juice, as the name implies, might become part of a passionate punch along with a hint of vanilla (an inspiring spice).

When you're pressed for time, there are several drinkables readily available to you with established meanings and attributes. *Note:* For those of you who prefer not to imbibe or who have allergies to alcohol, the nonalcoholic versions of beer, wine, and mead still retain their magical qualities.

These drinkables include:

READY-MADE BEVERAGE CORRESPONDENCES

Beer   purification, healing, blessing, promises and vows (solar)
Coffee   prayer, alertness, energy, socialization (solar)
Cider   health (solar)
Distilled beverages   banishing (solar)
Mead   eloquence, creativity, love, strength (lunar)
Milk   the mother aspect of the goddess, sustenance (lunar)
Tea   divination efforts, comfort, healing, courage (depends on base material)
Water   cleansing, purification, refreshment (lunar)
Wine   celebration, luck (red wine is solar)

Hint: Add some of these associations into the section that lists solar/lunar correspondences in your Book of Shadows.

To this traditional list I would seriously recommend adding other beverages that appear regularly on supermarket shelves so your spellbook is timely. Examples of these types of beverages include soda pop (for energy or joy), fruit juice (vitality, health), and flavored mineral water (varies by type).

Beverages in Spellcraft and Ritual

Once you find or prepare a beverage with magic in mind, the next question becomes one of how to use it. You'll want to note applications somewhere in this section of your Book of Shadows, perhaps in list format. The ideas here will get you started.

In spellcraft, potions are usually drunk by the creator or a group to internalize and integrate the associated energies. It is considered bad form, though, to give a magical beverage to anyone who does not know the purpose of what they're consuming. This is also true of food magic, especially since you're often making edibles for others. *Hint:* If you have an ethics portion to your spellbook, you might want to copy these guidelines into it.

There are some types of spellcraft where a beverage isn't wholly consumed. For example, a healing mixture that's partially consumed, while the rest is held in hand to absorb the malady. These remnants get poured out or dispersed to symbolically banish the problem.

Other ways to enhance the meaning behind a magical beverage include the following (*Hint:* You may want to cross-reference this section in the spellcraft section of your Book of Shadows):

• Freezing the beverage to symbolically cool, slow, or halt a specific type of energy (represented by the beverage's components).
• Heating the beverage for more active, passionate energy.
• Boiling the beverage to release its energy into the air via vaporization. Note that the remaining liquid will no longer be magically potent.
• Diluting the beverage to decrease or disperse a specific form of energy.
• Using a concentrated beverage to focus and augment power.

In a ritual context, beverages find still more functions! They can:

• Be poured out as a libation or offering to the god/dess. Just try to choose a suitable beverage for the deity being honored. Ideas along these lines can be found in chapter 13.
• Be used to represent the Water element. *Hint:* This option in the elemental section of your spellbook.
• Be used to mark the perimeter of the magic circle. *Note:* Try to make this a mixture that's good for the soil.

- Be used as a thematic drink consumed by all participants, which also symbolizes unity. This is seen commonly at initiations or coming of age rites where a specially prepared wine, aged a year and a day, is shared. *Hint:* This information in the ritual portion of your spellbook under scripting ideas.
- Be used to sprinkle the sacred space or participants. (Water is the most common beverage used for this application.)
- Be created in the sacred space for use at next year's gathering or to pass out to the participants as a take-home blessing.

Soul Food

As mentioned earlier this section, nearly every fruit, vegetable, meat, and spice on this planet has been categorized for its mystical energies. Since I can't be in your kitchen to know what you use most often, I've provided a list of books at the end of this chapter that will help you compile a list of food correspondences for your spellbook. You'll want to refer to these books to expand and diversify what I've been able to assemble here for you, and to get some alternative perspectives.

This section provides some listings to get you started, as were provided for the beverages mentioned earlier this chapter. The difference here is that, until recent years, people didn't really have food other than what they grew, and bread, eggs, and dried meat or fruit. So, I've adapted the concept a bit to include a few of the pre-prepared foods (or components) that we purchase instead.

READY-MADE FOOD CORRESPONDENCES

Animal crackers   internalizing animal attributes, way to honor a totem or familiar

Apple sauce   peace, love, health (may vary if flavored with a specific fruit)

Baking soda   increasing energy

Beef jerky   abundance, money

Bread   providence, prosperity, luck

Cake mix   wish magic, celebration

Cereal   Earth magic, money, grounding, protection *Note:* Any fruit
or sweetening in the cereal will change its potential application.

Chocolate   love, passion, life's sweetness

Corn   longevity, the Wheel of Time

Dried fruit   varies by type

Eggs   fertility, potential, metaphysical awareness

Instant breakfast   faster manifestation, energy

Jelly   joy, abundance (varies slightly by type)

Peanut butter   the god aspect, Earth magic, tenacity

Potatoes   healing, stability, Earth magic

Pretzels   cycles, the solar wheel

Salad croutons   alternative for breadlike energy

Tomato paste   smoothing love's path

How did I arrive at these correspondences? Through a combi-
nation of folklore and gut instinct, to be honest. Take the tomato
paste as an example. Here, the main ingredient is tomatoes, which
are a love food. The smashing and blending makes for congruity
and a smooth texture, therefore "smoothing love's path"!

Foods in Spellcraft and Ritual

As with beverages, most foods prepared for a spell get eaten to
best utilize the energy. There are some alternatives, however, like
baking a wishful bread and feeding it to the birds so they carry
your desire throughout Creation. And, as with beverages, the way
you prepare the food can affect its symbolic value. The only problem here is that most recipes have pretty specific mixing and cooking instructions so that the food comes out edible. So, add
preparation variations only when they won't affect the recipe's success. In this case, freezing, heating, and boiling have the same symbolic value as they do for beverages. Here are some more cooking
correspondences to copy into your Book of Shadows:

• Baking brings a slow release or augmentation of energy (this
seems especially suited to love magic).

- Drying preserves the energy and it's a good process to consider when you want to make self-regulatory foods since it has ascetic overtones.
- Chopping disperses energy into small, consumable portions for even distribution throughout the food.
- Sautéing adds a gentle quality to your magic, flavoring it lightly with energy from the item sautéed.
- Steaming brings crisp, stimulating energy (don't overdo it or all you'll get is soggy magic).

Basically, all you need to consider is exactly how the culinary process affects the food, and you'll understand how it will affect your magic too!

Eat, Drink, and Be Merry

Kitchen magic can be really fun as a way to preface or complete special gatherings. In this case you'll be making entire menus suited to the occasion based on the magical correspondences for the recipes (or their ingredients). Since these menus will vary dramatically depending on personal tastes, dietary restrictions, and the festival, I'm going to supply just a few samples here that you can use as a guideline in assembling menus for your spellbook.

Love Menu

Ideal for Valentine's day, anniversary celebrations, or any ritual aimed at improving the group's affinity towards one another.

Appetizer   tomato basil soup with shredded cheese
Vegetable   sweet potatoes with vanilla and brown sugar
Main dish   lemon chicken with pine nuts
Dessert   gingerbread or strawberry shortcake

Psychism Menu

Ideal for Samhain, Lammas, as preparation to divination efforts, or when contacting spirits.

Appetizer   dandelion salad with a sprinkling of fresh thyme
Vegetable   celery-stuffed mushrooms
Main dish   stir-fried tofu and crab with soy sauce and garlic (this adds protection to the blend)
Dessert   fried cakes with rose honey or coconut cream pie

Luck Menu

Ideal for St. Patrick's Day, May Day, most spring festivals, and any time your group needs a little improved good fortune.

Appetizer   stuffed cabbage leaves or dim sum
Vegetable   black-eyed peas with mint
Main dish   sausage-rice casserole
Dessert   sliced bananas with chopped hazelnuts, a fresh sprinkling of coconut, and heavy cream (add green food coloring to the cream to emphasize luck)

It's easy to see that your options in menu planning are as wide-ranging as the cookbooks you have on hand, and your own culinary skills. However, if you're not a great cook I wouldn't sweat it. Buy preprepared foods and beverages that suit the occasion, bless and energize them, then eat expectantly. Remember, folk magic works based on your heart's intention, not the complexity of preparations.

Suggested Reading

A Kitchen Witch's Cookbook. Patricia Telesco. St. Paul, Minn.: Llewellyn, 1994.

The Magic in Food. Scott Cunningham. St. Paul, Minn.: Llewellyn, 1991.

Compendium of Herbal Magick. Paul V. Beyerl. Custer, Wash.: Phoenix, 1998.

Personal Notes

_____

_____

_____

_____

_____

_____

_____

_____

_____

_____

_____

_____

_____

_____

10

Color, Sound, Texture, Aromatic, and Number Correspondences

Throughout the process of creating your Book of Shadows, you've probably noticed that symbolism is a key ingredient to all magical methods. You've probably also noticed that colors, textures, numbers, and other sensual dimensions have the capacity to improve the outcome of your magic incrementally. So, while some sections of your spellbook are dedicated to procedural examples and outlines, others review innermost feelings, and others, still, contain Wiccan theology, many sections will have simple correspondence lists. These lists create a foundation of information that you can refer to again and again in designing personal magics, or adapting those found in books.

To help this process along, this chapter will review the use of color, sound, textures, aromatics, and numbers as symbolic elements in magic. Of these, only the number section doesn't directly cue a sensual response. However, there are ways to blend numeric symbolism with the other types given here for potent results. So, I've included all these charts together (which also provides an easy reference that you can copy as desired into your Book of Shadows).

Color

Color directs the energy in our mind, with or without our knowledge that it does so. For example, watch the way children react to brightly painted rooms versus darker, more somber wall paint hues. You'll notice their energy changes. That's because the predominant color around us dramatically effects our moods, thoughts, and vitality. And, since color is marvelously subtle (i.e., it doesn't scream of magic to anyone looking), it provides us with an amazing array of potential private and meaningful magical applications including:

- Wearing specially colored clothes to change the vibrations we carry in our auras daily. (If you combine this with charged aromatics the results can be rather dramatic.)
- Adding specific colors into visualizations.
- Choosing a spell's components by color symbolism.
- Adding highlights of thematic color into the ritual space.
- Lighting our magical work space with colored lightbulbs or candles (and other accents) whose hue matches present intentions.
- Making magical foods and beverages whose colors reflect our goals.
- Adding coloring to aromatic oils or tinctures so both the scent and tint mirror the magic being created.
- Painting an altar cloth with suitably colored symbols during a ritual to match the magical intention. This cloth can be used again for the same purpose. Each time you use it, paint more emblems on it to saturate the cloth with energy. *Hint:* Copy this idea into either the tools section or the ritual section of your Book of Shadows.
- Using two-toned curtains around or near the sacred space to mark the division between world and not-world. *Note:* Black

and silver make for a neat effect, taking participants from darkness into light.

This last idea brings up an important point: the shade of a particular color is important. Bright, vibrant, clean hues accent similar types of active energy. Their crispness presents a clear purpose
to both the universe and your subconscious. Darker colors settle
and ground things, accenting a more restful state. Muddied hues
aren't very good for magic unless the color is being used as a substitute for an item (like mustard yellow being used when no mustard seed is present for a spell).

For the purpose of your spellbook, I suggest keeping a list of
rainbow color associations, and other in-between hues that you see
or use regularly. You can always blend two or more colors together
into spell components or ritual decorations to likewise blend the
vibrations generated by each. Here's a list of general correspondences to get you started:

MAGICAL COLOR CORRESPONDENCES

Hint: You might want to add chakra and astrological correspondences to this list.

Red   Energy, the Fire element, passion, love, power, life's
essence (blood), courage, stamina, summer magic, protection, Sun
and Fire magic.

Orange   Kindness, reaping what you've sown, friendship, the
season of fall, willfulness, awareness, Sun and Fire magic (less
"hot" than red, however).

Yellow (or Gold)   Solar magic, leadership, productivity, blessing, health. Vibrant yellow is a Fire color while pale yellow
corresponds to Air and matters of creativity, charisma, or communication.

Green   Healing, hope, growth. Dark green encourages fertility,
while ivy green stresses the emotions and sprout green accents
vitality and steady progress. An Earth color.

Blue Truthfulness, peace, joy. Light blue is a patient color, while dark blue supports dream magic. A Water color.

PURPLE Wisdom, spirituality, higher learning. Violet represents our connection to the higher self and Spirit, while lilac is more whimsical: the vibrant inner child. A Water color.

Black Banishing, rest, tenacity and constancy. An Earth color. The Void.

White (Silver) Purity, the Moon and the Goddess. A spirit color, also sometimes associated with Water (like the crest of a wave) or Air (blue-white).

Pink A quieter version of red, this color represents kind feelings, either friendly or romantic, or inner peace. It's a blend of Fire and Air energies.

Brown An earthy tone that represents grounding and foundations.

Gray The color of uncertainty. Poised between light and dark, grey represents neutral energy and perhaps the need to make a choice.

Sounds

While you might not immediately think of sounds as bearing symbolic value, they do. Some sounds have been with us since humankind's earliest history, making our reaction to them nearly instinctual. For example, when we hear a wild animal growling our immediate response is to fight or flee. The symbolic value of this sound is fear, caution, or preparedness. In considering the use of sounds for spells, rituals, and meditations, you'll want to keep these kinds of reactions in mind. Here is a brief list of sound associations:

SOUND CORRESPONDENCES

Classical music Tradition, legacies; color—dark green
Bells Protection, messages, focus; color—silver or gold
Chimes Time, cycles, omens; color—pale yellow or gold

Clapping   Excitement, happiness; color—bright orange

Crackling   Fire element, energy; color—blue (as with lightning or very hot fires) or red

Drumming   Safety, trance, communication, shamanic work, luck; color—red

Echo   Omens and signs, surrounding yourself with energy; color—grey

Gong   color—white-silver

Humming   Shifting vibrations, heightening energy; color—low pitched, brown, high pitched, green

Rain Stick   Water element, peace, harmony; color—blue

Religious Music   Faith, inspiration, color—purple

Silence   Introspection; color—pastels or white

Song   Appeasing the gods, emotional expression

Tambourine   Spirit communication; color—silverish

Trumpet   Announcements, the four elements; color—brass

Vowels   Toning, mantras, chanting

Wind chimes   Air element, fairies; color—pale blue

Make sure to add your own feelings to this list when copying it into your spellbook. You may also wish to cross-reference part of this list with colors and chakaras.

So, the next question becomes: How can you apply sounds to magical constructs? Well, here are some ideas that I hope will inspire more ideas for your Book of Shadows:

- Use a sound to send magic on its way or to activate it. For example, a bell could signal the release of a spell. In this case, you might change your incantation so it ends with something like *"hear my words, and heed them well, guide this magic when I sound this bell."* By changing the wording from *"guide"* to *"release"* the bell could then be used in the future to trigger the previously established energy parameter.

Hint: Copy this previous concept into the spellcraft section of your book.

- Use sound as a focusing tool in ritual or meditation. Gongs and drums in particular seem to fill this function. *Hint:* You may want to add these instruments to your list of tools.
- Use sharp sounds to release the cone of power during a ritual (this helps "cut" the magic and send it on its way).
- Use sounds to announce the opening or closing of a festival or observance. This helps separate the temporal and spiritual worlds and literally sets a tone for the event.
- Use sound (specifically music) as an extra thematic dimension that creates the right ambiance for any magical procedure.
- Use the sounds of nature as guides that provide cues for forthcoming weather patterns, or to answer questions on your mind (omen and sign observation).
- Use loud sounds to banish negativity and chase away malicious or mischievous spirits.
- Listen to the sounds produced by other people's magic or their auras to know their intention, or recognize people whose energy mingles well with your own.

Textures

Not everyone is as strongly affected by sound or sight as they are by the feel of something. When you put on a soft, fuzzy shirt, for example, it inspires a sense of coziness and comfort. These are the kinds of textural responses you'll want to consider adding into your magic. Mind you, these responses can be quite varied from person to person, so the associations I'm providing are rough generalizations at best (forgive the pun).

TEXTURAL CORRESPONDENCES

Bumpy   Distraction or difficulty, communication (braille)
Cold   Emotional distance, halting unwanted energies
Defined Edges   Boundaries, personal space
Hard   Sternness, austerity, security

Hot   Increasing energy and attention
Itchy   Distress, lies, anxious energy
Jagged   Caution, harshness, anger
Prickly   Overly protective, on guard, defensiveness
Rough   Antisocial tendencies, rigorous energy, a rogue
Smooth   Gentle nature, well-being, harmony
Soft   Kindness, sensitivity, possibly weakness
Sticky   Attraction and connection, deception

Here are some ideas on how textures can be applied to magical practices:

- Use a specific texture of cloth in creating pouches for divination tools.
- Use a symbolic texture of cloth in creating sachet-styled fetishes, charms, amulets, and talismans.
- Wear ritual clothing whose textures somehow represent the goal of the gathering (like wearing diaphanous clothing at a spring ritual to honor the Air element).
- Touch a thematic texture when casting a spell to add an extra sensual dimension.
- Use textures blended with color to represent the elements on your altar or to add to the Quarter points of a ritual.
- Add textural cues into your visualizations to make them more multidimensional (and therefore more effective).
- Sense the texture in other people's auras to know if you can work harmoniously with them. (Extend your senses toward the other person. What do you feel? Does their aura itch, feel sticky? Or is it smooth and comfortable? You probably won't be able to work effective magic with the itchy or sticky person.)

Aromatics

The metaphysical correspondence for a flower, herb, fruit, resin, and the like can (and often does) change when you consider it from a purely aromatic viewpoint. Why? Because the Air element gives movement to the energy, and changes its vibrations slightly. So, don't be overly confused when you read books on aromatherapy that note different capabilities for a scent than what you've read about an herb itself.

Here's a brief list of the magical associations for some popular aromatics to get your Book of Shadows started.

AROMATIC CORRESPONDENCES

Hint: Cross-reference these with the elemental portion of your Book of Shadows.

ACTIVITY

In adding more fragrances to this list, you can try a very simple exercise. Take out a bunch of spices, fruits, and other items from around your house. Close your eyes and randomly choose one (or have a friend put it under your nose). Smell deeply and see what word or phrase comes immediately to mind. This is the characteristic you should note in your spellbook!

Anise (Air element)   psychic insight
Basil (Fire element)   harmony
Berry (Water element)   joy, happiness, freedom
Cedar (Fire element)   bravery
Cinnamon (Fire element)   good fortune
Cloves (Fire element)   affection returned
Dill (Fire element)   stress reduction
Ginger (Fire element)   power, stamina
Lavender (Air element)   rest
Lime (Fire element)   turning negativity (especially thoughts)
Nutmeg (Fire element)   meditative focus
Orange (Fire element)   peaceful acceptance
Pine (Air element)   cleansing, money
Rose (Water element)   love

Rosemary (Fire element)   health and banishing
Sandalwood (Water element)   vitality and spirituality
Vanilla (Water element)   passion

Numbers

Rounding out our lists of correspondences for this section, we come to numbers. In ancient times, people used the art of numerology to determine all kinds of things including how many ingredients to use in healing a patient, or when to hold an important gathering. Additionally, the numbers involved in one's date and hour of birth were said to determine various things, like whether you could see ghosts. *Hint:* Cross-reference this information in the divination section of your spellbook.

Adding symbolic value to magical methods isn't difficult at all. Consider some of these options when you're working on your Book of Shadows or filling out its pages:

1. Preparing a specific number of foods to symbolize the energy created in a magical meal, or mixing a recipe a set number of times to slowly build supportive power.
2. Using a specific number of components to augment the symbolism of a spell, charm, amulet, or talisman. *Hint:* Points no. 1 and no. 2 work when making paper for your spellbook, too (see the recipe on page 6).
3. Having a certain number of people at a ritual to accent the gathering's theme.
4. Repeating a spell or the incantation in the spell a representative number of times.
5. Moving around the sacred circle a predetermined number of times to build a strong foundation for the cone of power. *Hint:* Copy this idea into the Wheel of Life section of your book.
6. Folding the paper or cloth in an amulet, charm, talisman, or fetish a symbolic number of times during the creation process. (*Hint:* Copy this idea into the Portable Magic section of your spellbook.)

7. Meditating or praying for a set number of hours or minutes preceding a magical procedure.

FOOD FOR THOUGHT

If you can't enact a spell at the time designated, what about substituting numerical symbolism instead? For example, if a spell calls for working at two A.M., perhaps you could use two main spell components or repeat the spell twice. Copy this concept into the spellcraft portion of your book.

Here are some numerical correspondences to get you started. You may wish to augment these with colors, chakras, gods and goddesses, cultural variations, and the like when transferring them into your spellbook. Also consider cross-referencing this information in the divination section of your Book of Shadows under the subheading "Numerology," if you have one.

Zero The unknowable, the magic circle, the Void or Ether, the moment before the "Big Bang," potential.

One The self, singularity of mind and purpose, the Sun, beginnings.

Two Partnership, duality for boon or bane, truth and beauty in balance.

Three Harmony, body-mind-spirit in symmetry, the trinity (maiden, mother, crone or son, father, grandfather), fate and manifestation.

Four Earth, the four corners of creation, the elements, stability and completion.

Five Protection, accountability, the pentagram.

Six Creativity, safety, dedication.

Seven The Moon, synchronicity, psychism.

Eight The Wheel of Time, reincarnation, authority, transition.

Nine Matters of law, grace, fulfillment.

Ten Follow through, precision.

Eleven   The emotions, our higher self.
Twelve   Concessions, cleansing, abundance.
Thirteen   The complete moon cycle, tenacity, a covenstead, luck.

Hint: In numerology, the symbolism of any number can be boiled down to one or two digits. To accomplish this, simply add each digit together. For example, if the number 24 keeps appearing in your life, 2 + 4 = 6, or the number that indicates the need for devotion, more caution, or an inspired streak. The method works with any date, address, and even license plates!

Suggested Reading

Folkways: Reclaiming the Magic and Wisdom. Patricia Telesco. St. Paul, Minn.: Llewellyn, 1995.

Healer's Handbook. Patricia Telesco. York Beach, Maine: Samuel Weiser, 1997.

Funk and Wagnall's Standard Dictionary of Folklore, Mythology, and Legend. San Francisco: Funk and Wagnall, 1972. Though this title is out of print, you may be able to find it in a good used book store.

Personal Notes

_____

_____

_____

_____

_____

_____

_____

_____

_____

_____

_____

_____

_____

_____

11

Crystals, Metals, Mineral, and Fossil Correspondences

The modern love of the earth's treasures is nothing new. In humankind's ancient past, we find people using all manner of stones to heal, protect, please the gods, mark sacred sites, and much more. This means there's a tremendous repository of folklore and mythology for the modern Witch to draw upon in designing this section of his or her Book of Shadows. Just go to your library and check out the collections of superstition and folklore in the reference section alone.

Exactly how deeply you explore the subject is really up to you. I do, however, recommend including some cultural variations in your correspondences to reflect humankind's diversity. I also recommend searching out astrological and planetary associations, chakra correlations, and divine beings to whom various stones were sacred. I've found having this kind of information in my spellbook has helped me tremendously in any number of magical procedures. (More on this will be discussed later in this chapter.)

What I'm going to provide here is some basic information about the earth's gifts to us that you will need to understand *any* magic in which you choose to use these items. Meditate on what's given here, then decide what is best to keep in your Book of Shadows for future reference.

Projective Versus Receptive

Stones contain two foundational types of energy: attractive/projective or receptive. Attractive/projective stones correspond to the god aspect, the Sun, and the athame. (*Hint:* Consider noting this association under tools.) Attractive/projective stones bear active energy, which is excellent for protective magic, improved fortune, strengthening will, and increasing success.

Some examples of common attractive/projective stones include amber, carnelian, bloodstone, quartz, flint, garnet, and tiger's-eye. Among metals and minerals we find gold, brass, aluminum, pyrite, tin, and iron. Carrying or wearing these stones keeps their energy with you. There's no need to "activate" the power—it simply radiates around the stone no matter where it may be.

Receptive stones correspond to the goddess aspect, the Moon, and the chalice. Receptive stones either (a) absorb specific types of energy easily or (b) increase our personal receptiveness. This makes them excellent for magic centered on inner peace, spirituality, banishing anxiety, psychic dreaming, and relationships.

Good examples of receptive stones include lace agate, amethyst, beryl, coral, rose quartz, fossils, jade, and turquoise. Among metals and minerals we find silver, copper, mercury, and lead. Receptive stones work most effectively when activated somehow. Holding the item, rubbing it in your hand or against your body, charging it with an incantation, and other similar methods are all ways of "waking up" the receptive stone's power. *Hint:* When creating your stone/metal correspondence lists, add your impressions of the stone's basic activeness or inactive traits.

I should mention at this point that some stones, even those given previously, defy categorizing. Many stones have mineral deposits or even bits of metal mixed in that can dramatically change their overall energy. So, I highly advocate treating each stone like an individual whose vibrations you have to get to know better in order to use it effectively in your magic.

STONE ATTUNEMENT EXERCISE

This activity is one that I find particularly useful in getting to know the stones I've chosen for magical work. Try it, and if you find it's successful for you too, copy it into your Book of Shadows.

Cup the chosen stone/metal in the palm of your projective hand (Your receptive hand is one you naturally use to accept a gift) and close your eyes. Breathe deeply, extending all of your senses toward the stone. Open all your spiritual awareness to feel and hear the stone's vibrations. (This often manifests as heat, static, or musical tones.) Make a mental note of any impressions you get.

Next, move the stone to your receptive hand. Wait patiently to see if you get a word or image from the stone that will help you determine its use later. Also take note of how the stone makes you feel. Do you feel grounded? Energized? Alert? Introspective? These are also important clues to the stone's basic matrix.

When you're done, make notes of your experience in the Magical Diary portion of your spellbook. Refer to them any time you want to use that particular stone in magic.

Color and Its Meaning

Hint: If you have a special section in your spellbook for metaphysical or holistic healing methods, you may want to cross-reference some of this information there since crystals have a long history of use in folk medicine.

If you've been following along with the order of this book, you already have a section on color symbolism set up in your spellbook. However, you should know that some slight variations exist between a color's general metaphysical correspondences and those associated with stones and their applications. This section will provide some more concrete ideas about using a stone's color to energize your magic based on traditional stone practices. Copy those you find most appealing into your Book of Shadows.

RED   Generally red stones are considered active, and useful in healing, bravery, augmenting willpower, and overall energy boosts. In ancient times, any stone of this color was regarded as a good ward against poison, mischievous fairies, and injury by fire. In matters of health, the ancients applied red stones for any blood disorders and "hot" maladies like rashes.

YELLOW   Yellow stones house the power of the Sun or Air, depending on the depth of color. Bright golden yellow accents the conscious, logical mind while pale yellow represents the Air element, and therefore matters of communication. In ancient times, yellow stones were carried to increase happiness, to cure jaundice, or aid digestive difficulties.

GREEN   Green stones, specifically moss agate, were a great boon to gardeners, being used to promote crop growth and healthy soil. Carrying a green stone also draws money to you and a little extra luck. For health, green stones were thought to aid eyesight and allay headaches.

BLUE   Blue is a very receptive color and is thought to promote peace and restfulness, which may be why some blue stones were used as protection against nightmares. They're also particularly helpful in achieving trance states. In healing, blue stones are said to reduce pain and generally help in getting a difficult patient to sleep.

BLACK   Black stones have traditionally been used as "worry" stones, neatly collecting negativity into their frame. For this reason, they're often seen in banishing techniques. Besides this, black stones have strong Earth energies that help keep our feet on the ground.

PURPLE   Purple is receptive. Almost universally, purple stones have been applied to spiritual matters and self-rulership. It is for this reason that parents sometimes gave children purple stones (amethyst in particular) to encourage obedience. They're also excellent for bolstering faith. For health, these stones have traditionally be used to allay melancholy, promote rest, and ease headaches.

WHITE (SILVER)   These stones are lunar and receptive, and have strong Goddess associations. As a result, women often carried white stones during or after pregnancy to ensure a healthy child and flowing milk. Magically, white stones appear frequently in luck-drawing activities, and as amulets for protection on the road. *Hint:* Consider adding this last concept into the section on portable magic in your spellbook.

The Selection Process

Go to gem and mineral shows, contact the geology department at a nearby university, check out science shops and New Age stores. These places will have a variety of stones in an equally diverse range of prices. Know, however, that the price of a stone doesn't necessarily equate to quality or usefulness. *Hint:* This is true of all magical tools. While the ancients did value precious substances as being more effective in magic because of their purity, minor flaws will not make or break your methods. In fact, it may be the flaws or other minerals present in a stone that enhance a specific type of energy flow.

So, how do you know which stone to pick? I take my cue from my kids. I love watching them play with the stones in the bins at New Age shops. They intuitively know which ones they need at the moment, and find tremendous joy in the discovery process. As adults, however, our ability to respond instinctively to stones sometimes gets tarnished with logical, right-brain thinking. To know which stones are best for your personal "kit," or for a specific purpose, we have to rediscover the inner child who knows how to simply *feel*.

Here is one way that I find stones myself. Try it out when you get a chance. If it helps you, copy it into your Book of Shadows to use again:

Stand in front of the stones from which you must choose. Put out your strong hand (the one you write with), palm down over the selection. Take a deep, cleansing breath, close your eyes, and focus on the use you have in mind. Now, simply feel the energy emanating from the stones. As you pass your hand over them, you should sense one drawing you, or perhaps a tingling in your palm. This usually indicates the best choice for your goal. If the stone is too expensive for your budget, appeal to the universe for a way to obtain it (perhaps through barter or trade).

The Correspondences

This list provides the groundwork for the one that you will be putting in your Book of Shadows. For the purpose of brevity and usability, I've focused mostly on the metals, stones, and crystals that are readily available. You will probably want to add in gem-stones, birthstone correspondences, religious significance (if applic-able), weekday and hour associations, and historical and cultural information as you find it, so leave plenty of room for extra asso-ciations. *Hint:* Cross-reference some of the following information with the god/goddess section of your spellbook.

Stone	Magical Correspondences
Agate	Clear speech, the conscious mind, honesty, love, success, protection. *Note:* The color of the agate and the patterns on its surfaces will vary its application greatly.
Amber	Fire and Sun magic, healing, safety. The least expensive source for amber is bead shops.
Amethyst	Self control, business savvy, psychism, encouraging visionary dreams. Suitable offering for Bacchus.
Bloodstone	Turning anger, good fortune, weather magic, divination (omens), truth seeing.
Copper	Gathering and transmitting energy, focus.
Coral	Protection from wounds, sagacity, water magic, appeasing sea spirits.

Stone	*Magical Correspondences*
Flint	Protection from fairies, harvesting magical herbs.
Fossils	The primal self, past life regression, increased mystical energy and protection.
Gold	The Sun and god aspect, reason, the conscious mind, victory.
Hematite	Magnetism, charm, aiding with legal problems. A suitable offering to Mars.
Iron	Commitment, strength, protection.
Jade	Love, devotion, weather magic, good fortune. Sacred to Buddha.
Jet	Safety, banishing nightmares, gardening magic. Prayer sacred to Cybele.
Lapis	Spiritual leadership, joy, a helpmate to healing and meditation.
Lead	Grounding.
Meteorites	The divine hand in human affairs, safety when carried, vitality-inspiring.
Moonstone	Fortune-telling, moon magic, smoothing love's path, peaceful sleep. Sacred to most moon goddesses (Selene is one).
Onyx	Spirit control, turning unwanted attentions.
Pumice	Easing childbirth, banishing negativity or unwanted emotions, overcoming.
Pyrite	The true self, fortune-telling, protection.
Quartz	A stone that readily accepts whatever energy you charge it with. A quartz point can become an alternative wand for directing energy during rituals and spellcraft. (*Hint:* Cross-reference this concept under tools.)
Salt	Protection, the Earth element, foundations, prosperity. Sacred to Aphrodite.
Silver	The Moon and the goddess, intuitive senses.
Tiger's-Eye	Courage, safety, playfulness, prosperity.
Tin	Luck.
Turquoise	Bravery, prosperity, kinship, improved fortune, protection from accidents. Sacred to Hathor and Buddha.

Applications

Now comes the fun part—putting it all together into a functional construct. Stones and metals represent some of the most durable and diversified components for your magic. As such, you're going to want to give them a little extra space in your spellbook, especially under sample applications. Here are just a few examples of the ways in which I use stones from the notes in my own Book of Shadows. Take what you like and use it to begin this section in your spellbook.

Charms, Amulets, Talismans, and Fetishes

From a purely traditional standpoint, stones were among the most popular components for these tools in nearly all cultural settings. So, you may want to cross-reference some stone associations in this section of your spellbook. When used for portable magic, the stone was either carved, painted, energized with an incantation, carried on one's person or in a medicine bundle, and the like.

Divination

For scrying and cast systems, crystals are wonderful. They attract your attention through their beauty, and help improve concentration. You can choose scrying stones for their symbolic value or clarity, while casting stones should be chosen for what you want them to represent in the system. *Hint:* Add this last idea to the divination section of your spellbook.

Elemental Representations

Around the home or in the sacred space, stones and metals make lovely representatives of the elemental world through either (a) their traditional associations or (b) color.

Healing

Crystal healing has become more popular in modern times, but its methods are very ancient. The idea here is that the wavelength at which a crystal vibrates can (and does) change the auric envelope around a person's body, and therefore helps with overall wellness. Exactly which crystals get used and how they are used depends greatly on the healer.

Honoring Patron or Patroness Deities

Stones, and especially gems, have long been used to honor and appease the gods. Just make sure the stone you choose somehow represents the deity whose attention you're trying to get.

Indicating or Augmenting Ley Lines, Power Spots, and Vortexes

Looking to well-known sacred sites like Stonehenge, it becomes clear that the ancients used large stones to mark the earth's power network and there's no reason for us not to follow the example. Many sacred geometrists feel that doing so will help with Earth healing by reconnecting the lines of force that got disrupted with war, overpopulation, and development.

Marking the Sacred Circle

Along the same lines, since stones mark the earth's sacred places, why not also use them to mark your sacred circle. Lay out stones so they make the circular pattern, and maybe paint them in elemental colors to create a medicine wheel of force around yourself.

Meditation Aid

Place the chosen crystal on the chakra (energy center) of your body that most closely corresponds with your meditation's theme. For example, when trying to open psychic pathways, put a moonstone or something similar on your third eye (between the eyebrows).

Stone Spirits

Shamans feel that the spirits in stones can help us learn about, and intimately communicate with, the mineral realm. This practice takes time and effort, but will reveal many things about the best ways in which to use stones for daily magical practices.

Touch Stones

Touch stones are those that you literally touch to release their energy, sometimes while using an activating phrase. This can be done with any stone, but seems to work best with the receptive type.

Wish Magic

Last, but certainly not least, metals and minerals were used readily in wish magic. They were often tossed into a well or running water source as a gift to the spirits who abide there.

Care and Feeding

As with any magical tool, your metals, minerals, and crystals require care to function well in magic. When you first get any of these tools, clear them of any residual energies. Remember, a lot of people may have handled them before you, and you don't necessarily want or need those remnant vibrations influencing your magic. There are different ways of accomplishing a good cleansing, but the most popular by far is a simple cleansing with cool salt or lemon water. (You'll notice this in the tools section of your spellbook too). Note that you will likely have to repeat this procedure with the item after one, or several, uses.

Next comes charging. This basically hooks up the stone to spiritual energy flows, like a plug in an electrical outlet. In ancient times people even went so far as to feed crystals with animal blood to keep them vital. In modern times, most practitioners simply leave the item in sunlight or moonlight, visualize it being filled with radiance, place it in proximity with other energized crystals, or fill the stone using repeated incantations.

Whatever your personal choice, saturate the chosen metal or stone with the right type of power for the job you have at hand. For example, if you're working magic for the conscious mind, don't charge the stone in moonlight. The energy is contrary to your goal. As with cleansing, you'll likely need to recharge your crystals periodically as you use up the energy you've placed within them.

Finally, consider suitable storage for your metals and stones. Single-purpose stones don't require this because you're probably giving them back to the earth, or to a person, anyway. However, any items that you plan on using regularly for magic should have a safe place that keeps unwanted hands and "vibes" neatly away.

Suggested Reading

Curious Lore of Precious Stones. George Frederick Kunz. Dover, N.Y.: Dover, 1971.

Crystal, Gem, and Metal Magic. Scott Cunningham. St. Paul, Minn.: Llewellyn, 1995.

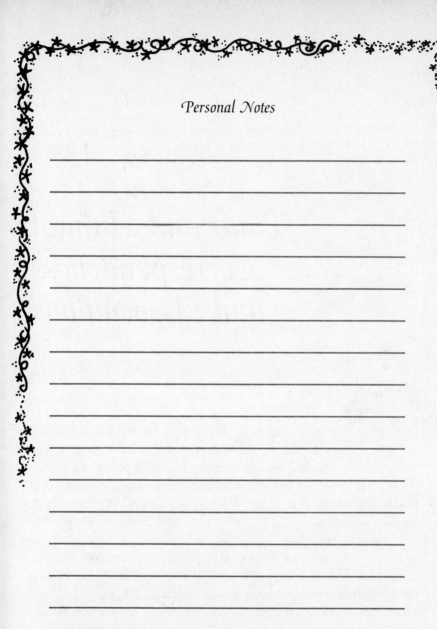

Personal Notes

12

Plant and Animal Correspondences and Associations

After reviewing all the magical potential in the mineral kingdom, we now move into the animal and vegetable realms. With urban sprawl slowly creeping into more and more wild places, it's harder today than it used to be to truly connect with nature. Nonetheless, this connection is vital to the Witch. The earth is our mother and a source for nurturing, so its citizens are well deserving of space in your Book of Shadows.

In considering how to organize this section, please bear in mind that the historical uses of plants and animals do not always match modern ones for two reasons. First we've become aware of toxicities, which is how we come by the herbalist's rule, "If one can cure, two can kill." Many plants that were once readily used in remedials are now left to more symbolic functions in the magic circle. *Reminder:* In magic, a symbol is no less potent than what it represents as long as you treat it respectfully.

Second, we're trying to be good stewards of the earth by not abusing its resources. So unlike the ancients, modern magical people don't offer up animal sacrifices or use animal parts (other than found ones) in their methods. Instead, we turn to creative alternatives, like carvings or other art forms. This knowledge will be important in adapting older spells so they mingle harmoniously with your Book of Shadows today and tomorrow.

Plants and Plant Parts

In many settings plants were regarded as having indwelling spirits. With proper growing, harvesting, and preparation techniques, one could tap into those spirits and manifest magic. Nearly every plant part (if not all) has been used in various types of mystical efforts from making a potion for star-crossed lovers to healing maladies, and everything in between!

This means that nature has (yet again) provided us with a rich repository of tradition and potential for our magical efforts. Consequently, your Book of Shadows should incorporate any trees, flowers, herbs, bushes, fruits, vegetables, roots, leaves, etc. that you feel you'll use regularly in your magical practice. And, just for fun and variety, include a few unusual ones too.

The following list will get you started with some plants or plant parts that are available around your home or on supermarket shelves. Remember when copying the entries into your spellbook to add things like astrological and planetary associations, gender associations, gods and goddesses to whom the plant was sacred, superstitions surrounding the plant that may affect its magical application, and any other interesting or useful correspondences you stumble across. Your options are nearly limitless!

Plant	Magical Applications
Alfalfa	Protection, providence.
Almond	Love, devotion. Sacred to Zeus.
Aloe	Beauty, luck, protection.
Anise	Purification, calling spirits. Sacred to Apollo and Mercury.
Apple	Health, longevity, devotion. Sacred to Diana and Odin (among others).
Ash	Luck, turning magic, vision. Sacred to Thor, Neptune, and Odin.
Banana	The god aspect, fertility, summerland rituals. Sacred to Kanaloa.
Basil	Devotion, fortune-telling, protection. Sacred to Vishnu and Krishna.
Bay	Strength, psychic awareness, healing. Sacred to Apollo and Fides.
Beans	Virility (male). A divinatory tool sacred to Hecate and Circe.
Blackberry	Joy, profuseness, fertility. Sacred to Brigit.
Cabbage	Good luck (especially for relationships).
Catnip	Love, comeliness, joy. Sacred to Bast.

Plant	Magical Applications
Celery	Balancing conscious and unconscious mind, clarity, insight.
Cinnamon	Victory, power, passion, safety, health. Sacred to Venus.
Clover	Luck, fidelity, turning hexes.
Coconut	The goddess or the Moon, prosperity. Sacred to Sri.
Corn	Fertility, providence, luck. Sacred to Demeter and Hades.
Cotton	Banishing spirits, weather magic.
Daisy	Divination, Sun magic. Sacred to Freya, Artemis, and Thor.
Dandelion	Oracular work, messages. Sacred to Hecate.
Dill	Protecting children, antimagic charm.
Elm	Fairy folk, love. Sacred to Odin.
Fig	Enlightenment, fertility, homecomings. Sacred to Bacchus, Buddha, and Mithra.
Garlic	Exorcism, protection, health. Sacred to Hecate.
Ginger	Energy, victory, love. Sometimes used to consecrate tools. (*Hint:* Cross-reference this use under tools.)
Grape	Completion, success, celebration. Sacred to Dionysus and Bacchus.
Hawthorn	Fairies, fecundity, devotion. Sacred to Flora and Bloddeuwedd.
Hazel	Wisdom, imagination, protection from lightning. Sacred to Mercury and Diana.
Horseradish	A fiery herb good for exorcism.
Lemon	Romance, passion, long life.
Lettuce	Well-being, rest, chastity.
Marigold	Psychism, legalities, dreams, cleansing.
Mint	Passion, protection, prosperity, purification, health. Sacred to Hades and Mintha.
Oak	Safety, well-being, fertility, fortune. Sacred to Janus, Jupiter, Cybele, and Zeus.
Olive	Fertility, blessing, prosperity. Sacred to Athena, Apollo, and Concordia.
Onion	Banishing, health, psychic dreams, vision. Sacred to Isis.
Orange	Fidelity, love, fortune-telling. Sacred to Apollo and Hera.
Peas	Divination, luck. Sacred to Nuba.
Peach	Wisdom, wishes, love.

Plant	Magical Applications
Pine	Turning magic, safety, cleansing, health. Sacred to Rhea, Poseidon, Pan, and Astarte.
Potato	The Earth element, healing. Alternative to a poppet. *Hint:* Put this in the tools section of your spellbook, or under spellcasting ideas.
Rice	Protection from evil, rain magic, fertility, providence, longevity. Sacred to Amaterasu.
Rose	Love, blessing, passion, psychic awareness. Sacred to Aphrodite, Venus, and Bacchus.
Sage	Cleansing, longevity, wish magic. Sacred to Jupiter and Zeus.
Sunflower	Solar and Fire magic, abundance, wishes. Sacred to Apollo and Demeter. *Hint:* Sunflower seeds are a good choice here.
Tomato	Love, protection.
Vanilla	Energy, alertness, love, clearing confusion.
Walnut	Fertility (male), the conscious mind. Sacred to Jupiter and Zeus.

Applications

So, what are some of the ways you can use this information? Hey, get creative! I can't honestly think of a magical process wherein you *can't* use plant matter. Here are some suggestions that you can put in your spellbook:

AROMATICS   Incense, potpourri, anointing oils, personal magical perfume, spirited rug and room fresheners, and mystical massage creams are the tip of the iceberg here. Using the scented components from nature and their associations, you can fill nearly any space with a true magical air!

SPELL COMPONENTS   Plants can be plucked, burned, buried, planted, watered, baked, and strewn as part of spellcraft. Picking gathers the energy, burning disperses it, burial engenders growth or banishing, planting also encourages maturation, and watering provides nurturing energy. Baking slowly increases power, nudging it toward manifestation (this, obviously, pertains to edible plants).

Activity

Save a bunch of dried fruit rinds (apple, orange, grapefruit, lemon, and lime). Cut these into one-inch squares and string them on long pieces of thread. Bless the bundle and hang it in a window to release cleansing, healthful, loving energies into your home. Grind little pieces up when you need some incense, or cut off a few pieces for simmering potpourri to quickly release magical power as needed.

Strewing releases the plant's energy to the winds. *Hint:* You may want to cross-reference these ideas in the spellcraft section of your book.

SACRED SPACE—INDOORS AND OUT   Within the home elementally aligned plants can become Quarter markers, as could any suitable aromatic plant part. For a circle, one might sprinkle flower petals or appropriate herbs around the circle to mark the line between the worlds. Outside, you can plant magical theme gardens for meditation, or even grow trees in a circular pattern to create a place for ritual.

HONORING THE DIVINE   Plants of all types, especially those used for food, or those known to be sacred to a specific divinity, appeared on altars around the world as offerings. We can certainly follow this custom when a ritual or spell seems suited to a gift of gratitude to the Powers of Creation for their assistance in our work. Plant offerings were often burned or consumed after a working, so you might want to choose edible offerings and then cook them for a thematic after-ritual feast! *Hint:* Add this idea into the food-beverage section of your spellbook, or perhaps the ritual section.

RITUAL TOOLS   Branches of trees and bushes, and fronds of various flowers make serviceable wands and aspergers tools in the sacred space. *Hint:* Add this option to your tool list.

MAGIC FOR GROWTH, GROUNDING, OR ROOTING   Plant a seed that represents your magical goal. By watering and tending it you help bring the energy to fruition. Also, if you name the seed "self" it can represent firm spiritual foundations. Alternatively you can name it after an attribute you want dispersed around the plant, like protection.

Once planted and tended, the protective energy takes root where you most need it. *Note:* This is a simple type of folk spell that can be augmented by an incantation that further delineates its purpose. You might want to copy it into the spellcraft section of your book.

HEALING   The ancient herbal healing methods are experiencing a tremendous revival, and there are hundreds of good books you can study on the subject. Just be aware that certain laws govern herbalism, and that it's best used as an adjunct to modern medicine unless you're very experienced in the art.

VISUALIZATION   Find a plant that represents your goal, then visualize it growing from a seed to fullness with your face superimposed over the main part (like the center of a flower or the top of a tree). *Hint:* Add these ideas to the meditation part of your Book of Shadows.

COMMUNING WITH PLANT SPIRITS   Plant spirits can teach us much about the earth and how to heal it (which indirectly helps heal humankind too). Just as you attuned yourself to stones in the last chapter, now you're going to readjust your spiritual antenna to the plant kingdom. To learn about and from a particular plant spirit, you should dedicate a specific amount of time to working with one or two specific species at the most. Make notes of the way they grow, their texture, aromas at different times of the day, how the plant takes to various elements, etc. Meditate with that plant nearby, and sleep with it next to your bed. Make sure to keep a tape recorder or paper and pen handy to note any telepathic messages or dream imagery that the plant gives you. *Hint:* This is an excellent idea for your dream diary too.

Plant Kingdom Helps and Hints

As an avid herbalist and someone who really enjoys using various plants in magic, I've discovered a few things that you might want to add to this section of your Book of Shadows. Namely:

• The fresher a plant (or a plant preparation) is the better it responds to magical energy, unless you leave the item where it will receive constant charging.

• Dry plants and plant parts are fine for convenience, but they don't have the magical vitality fresh ones do because the vital oils (and life energy) are also "dry." Mind you, there are cases when the dry quality may help your magic, such as when performing a good-weather spell! (*Hint:* Add this idea into the spellcraft section of your book.)

• The essential oil from a plant is a perfectly good substitute for fresh parts. Just be careful—these oils can be harsh on the skin, and some are toxic to pets.

• Growing your own magical plants and harvesting them at a traditional time (e.g., Midsummer's Day) does seem to boost the magical energy within. *Hint:* Add this information about Midsummer's Day into the holiday section, if you have one, of your spellbook.

• If you have to buy plants from a supplier, organic plants have the best magical potential (chemicals can obscure magical intention). Also, find a supplier you can trust. One green leafy thing looks a lot like another, and not all companies are honest in their packaging.

• Along the same lines, as you collect plants for magical work make sure to carefully label everything both inside and outside the container. Always trust the rule: If you're not sure what it is, don't use it!

Animals

In ancient times, certain animals were worshiped as divine or semi-divine entities. In addition, all kinds of animals were ritually offered to the gods or eaten so people could internalize the creature's attributes (like fish for fertility). Animal parts and images found their way into amulets and talismans, animal symbolism appeared in dream dictionaries and omen guides, and, today, magical practitioners often seek out spirit animals or have familiars as magical companions.

With all this in mind, you will want to have some type of animal correspondence list in your Book of Shadows that includes the different meanings and uses for the animal depending on the setting. For example, what a creature means in a dream can be drastically different from what its real life appearance means as an omen. In the examples I'm providing in this section, I've abstained from including dream imagery because that will be covered later in this book in the Magical Diary section. I've also limited this exploration to common totems or creatures (including insects) that are still regularly interacting with our society.

Your spellbook's entries can begin with these, which you can expand on as you find more animal associations. Remember to leave extra room between each entry to add cultural variants, omen and sign interpretations, planetary correspondences, amuletic uses, and the like. *Hint:* Cross-reference some of these with the god and goddess associations in your spellbook. Also, if you're a meat eater some of the consumable animals on this list might be added to the food magic section of your Book of Shadows!

Creature	*Associations*
Ant	Industry, community, craftsmanship.
Bat	Vision, the soul's journey.
Bear	Power, cycles, guardian energy. Sacred to Odin and Artemis.
Bees	Messages, communication, luck. Sacred to Venus.
Blue jay	Communication, magical mimicry, guardian energy.
Butterfly	Transformation, enlightenment, reincarnation. Sacred to the Horae.
Cat	Playfulness, equilibrium, grace. Sacred to Bast.
Chicken	Divination, fertility, health.
Cow	Prosperity, the goddess aspect. Sacred to Hathor.
Cricket	Luck, happiness, abundance, blessings.
Deer	Education (spiritual), security, gentility. Sacred to Artemis, Aphrodite, and Diana.
Dog	Service, trust, devotion, psychic vision.
Dolphin	Oracles, divine messages, the breath of life. Sacred to Apollo.
Fish	Fertility, perseverance, providence. Sacred to Oannes and Vishnu.

Creature	Associations
Fox	Invisibility, half-truths, quick action, shape-shifting. Sacred to Bacchus and Enki.
Frog	Fertility, health, honesty. Sacred to Hekt.
Hare	The Moon, fecundity. Sacred to Aphrodite and Eros.
Horse	Movement, fertility, divination. Sacred to Mars and Kwannon.
Lark	Cheerfulness, solar magic.
Mole	Revealing secret matters.
Mouse	Economy, getting around barriers. Sacred to Apollo.
Nightingale	Love, lightening burdens. Sacred to Adonis and Attis.
Owl	Self-truth, wisdom, vision. Sacred to Athena.
Pig	Renewal.
Raven	Prophesy. Sacred to Hellios.
Robin	Harbinger of spring, the Fire element. Sacred to Thor.
Snail	Birth, luck, divination. Sacred to Tecciztecatl.
Snake	Transformation, health. Sacred to Hermes, Ra and Hygeia.
Spider	Fate, destiny, networks. Sacred to Holda, the Norns, Spider Woman, and the Fates.
Squirrel	In-gathering, storage. Sacred to Medb.
Turtle	The earth, creativity, regeneration. Sacred to Vishnu, Hsi Wang-Mu, and Ea-Oannes.
Turkey	Charity, self sacrifice.
Whale	The Water element, rejuvenation, initiation. Sacred to many oceanic deities.

Applications

Bearing the symbolic animals in mind, the next question becomes one of application. Animals aren't quite as versatile for magic as plants, but they still have a fair number of uses. Here's some to consider for your spellbook:

VISUALIZATIONS   Seeing yourself turn into an animal, or accompanied by an animal is one way of drawing that creature's energies and characteristics into your life. You can also imagine the animal's image sinking into a suitable chakra, like an owl merging with your heart chakra when you need to be wise and honest in a relationship.

ANIMAL GUIDES   While this concept is more shamanic than Wiccan, there is a strong belief in the magical community that spiritual representatives of the animal kingdom come to individuals to offer aid and insight. Such a creature is often discovered by taking a middle-world trance journey, or it may reveal itself through a dream. *Hint:* Note this possibility in the dream journal section of your Magical Diary.

SPELLCRAFT   If an animal part comes to you, like finding a feather, it's perfectly acceptable to use it as a spell component since nature gifted you with it. When luck isn't with you, then you can use artistic renditions of animals instead. For example, a charm for strength might begin with a stone carving of a lion. Or, a spell to banish lies might begin with a picture of a fox that is burned or buried to destroy the dishonesty. *Hint:* Copy this idea into the spellcraft section of your book.

ELEMENTAL REPRESENTATIVES   Animal carvings, paintings, drawings, and photographs make excellent elemental markers in the sacred circle. In this case, however, rather than calling on the elements themselves, you might want to call spirit animal representatives to guard the circle! Briefly, here are some elemental associations for animals. *Hint:* You may want to add this into the animal correspondence list, the elemental list, or leave it as a separate chart.

ANIMALS AND THE ELEMENTS

Earth   Rabbit, deer, snake, mole, mouse, ground hog.
Air   Birds, butterfly, bee (also Fire). Many flying insects.
Fire   Desert-dwelling animals, lion, horse, electric eel (also Water), firefly (also Air).
Water   Duck, seal, dolphin, most fish, seahorse, beaver.

You can also use these associations in protecting your home. Just put an image of the creature you want to keep an eye on things somewhere near your threshold. Each day as you go out or come in, briefly thank the spirit for its diligent vigil.

FAMILIARS   Many people in the magical community have pets that they consider familiars—helpmates to magic and spiritual companions. Mind you, it seems that familiars choose their humans, not vice versa, so don't just go out and get a pet hoping for a familiar. If an animal comes to you and it shows an avid interest in your magic, this is a good sign. Over time you may discover an empathic connection with the animal that improves rapport, and slowly a familiar relationship will develop. Trust me when I say you'll know the difference between a familiar and a normal animal.

OMENS AND SIGNS   Last, but not least, magicians and diviners alike have oft depended on animal signs to know when the energies were most fortunate. There are thousands of animal omens and signs that you can find in any good collection of folklore. Here are but a few to get you started:

Ants (visible hills)   the weather will be fair
Cat (coming to you)   improved finances
Bees (flying near you)   a message or news en route
Birds (on the right or rising up)   a good sign
Canary (singing)   happiness
Cricket (entering the home)   improved luck or friendship
Dog Howling   generally a negative omen
Dove   the bearer of peace and happiness
Flies (biting)   rain is coming
Hare (meeting)   be careful
Hawk   presages victory over circumstances
Horse (seeing)   positive sign—the day will be good
Hummingbird   foretells love or improved relationships
Mice   trouble ahead
Moth (moving toward you)   a letter or message
Robin   visitors or improved fortune
Sparrow   domestic tranquility

Suggested Reading

Compendium of Herbal Magick. Paul V. Beyerl. Custer, Wash.: Phoenix, 1998.

Symbolic and Mythological Animals. J. C. Coopr. London: Aquarian, 1992. Though this title is out of print, you may be able to find it at a good used book store.

Animal-Speak. Ted Andrews. St. Paul, Minn.: Llewellyn, 1993.

The Herbal Arts. Patricia Telesco. Secaucus, N.J.: Carol Publishing Group, 1998.

Personal Notes

_____

_____

_____

_____

_____

_____

_____

_____

_____

_____

_____

_____

_____

_____

_____

_____

_____

13

God and Goddess
Correspondences

This part of your Book of Shadows should focus mostly on any patron gods or patroness goddesses you've chosen to follow. And since the potential choices number in the tens of thousands (literally), I won't presume to cover specific deities in detail here. Instead, this section is dedicated to giving you information for your Book of Shadows that can be applied to any god or goddess. I've also included a brief list of some deities that you may wish to explore further at some later date.

Choosing a God or Goddess

Not everyone who practices magic follows a specific god or goddess. In fact, not every magician figures the divine into the magical equation. However, considering the prevalence of gods and goddesses in the world's religious traditions, it is something well worth considering for yourself. If you find you're uncomfortable with integrating a sacred power into your personal path, then I suggest just keeping a small portion of your spellbook open for an identification list. This way, when you come across spells, chants, or rituals that have the names of gods and goddesses in them, you'll know what those powers represent.

If, on the other hand, you do want to have one or several divine beings that you work with regularly, going through the rest of this chapter will help you.

Personal Gods and Goddesses

There are many ways to choose gods and goddesses to feature in your Book of Shadows, and to follow personally. Perhaps there's a cultural context that's associated with your magical tradition that you can look to, or a tradition from your family's heritage. Maybe the name, symbol, or sacred animal of a god or goddess has come to you in a dream or appeared regularly in your life. Maybe there's a being that, for whatever reason, affects you on a deep, emotional level. Then too, there might be a god or goddess associated with your career, your art, your personality type, or whatever. All of these represent good places to begin your searching and spellbook notes.

If none of the aforementioned apply to you, try reading through some of the books listed at the end of this chapter, or talking to magical friends. Usually if you let the universe know what you're seeking, and you make an honest effort, a god/dess will make itself known to you somehow—and not necessarily the way you expect!

Alternative Gods and Goddesses

In working with the divine, you may discover some magical procedures are ill suited to a specific deity's talents and attributes as detailed in your Book of Shadows. When this happens, you can create and refer to an alternative god/dess list instead—one that catalogs deities, their cultural origin, and general characteristics. A good example of such a list is given at the end of this chapter.

Mind you, I don't advocate invoking a power to which you have no emotional-spiritual connection, or whose name you can't even pronounce. But, if you use your Book of Shadows listing as a basic reference, do some extra research into a helpful Divine persona's demeanor, and then honor him or her suitably in your sacred space, this is perfectly acceptable.

What to Include in Your Book of Shadows

Okay, say you or your group has chosen one or several gods and goddesses to call on regularly in magical workings and worship. Now what? How do you give such an expansive Power suitable space in your Book of Shadows, and what's best to include? That's not an easy question, and it has to be answered in part by your own heart. The way each person sees a god/dess is very personal. So, what's important about Thor to a specific individual, and what information about this deity gets detailed in that person's Book of Shadows, might vary dramatically from another person who also follows Thor.

Confused yet? Don't be. Here are some good guidelines that you can use in detailing your chosen deity or deities in the pages of your spellbook:

NAME   Hey, begin at the beginning! What's the name of the deity or Divine persona in question and how do you *correctly* pronounce that name? Why is pronunciation so important? Well, how do you feel when people say your name incorrectly? Since this god/dess is someone you want as an ally, it's considered polite and respectful to get the name right.

ACTIVITY

Look up the name of the god/dess you've chosen in a name book (like those for babies) and see what it means. Or do a little research into the original language in which the name appears to learn its translation. You'll often find this gives you important clues as to the god/dess' attributes, powers, or suitable offerings.

ATTRIBUTES   What characteristics or powers are most strongly associated with this Divine persona? For example, is he or she a god/dess of love? Health? Prosperity? After listing these primary attributes, also give yourself some information on secondary faculties, including those that may have changed over time, or when that god/dess was presented to another cultural group. *Note:* A god/dess' major attributes are those powers (love, health, joy, divination, or whatever) that characterize that deity. These are the attributes which you would generally call upon him or her for assistance with.

CULTURAL CONTEXT Where did this god/dess originate, and how did people in that time and place view him or her? To understand why this is so important, think about how people in your hometown know you better than "outsiders." Similarly, the cultural group in which a god/dess manifested itself will likely have unique and insightful outlooks about that Divine persona's myths, abilities, and demeanor.

DESCRIPTION How does this god/dess look? Is he or she old, young, handsome, plain, tall, short, etc.? The more descriptive you can get here, the better. It helps build a mental image which you can focus on later. It will also help you find a suitable depiction of him or her for your altar.

SACRED THINGS What animals, plants, aromatics, or people did this god/dess protect or love? Once you know this information you can adopt a similar outlook towards those things. Doing so honors that god/dess. Decorate your sacred space and altar with a few of these items too.

TRADITIONAL OFFERINGS In moments of great need what did people offer this god/dess and what happened to that offering afterward? For example, in some cultures offerings were burned so they could reach the divine. *Hint:* This gives the ritual fire another use that you might want to note under tools or ritual ideas. In other settings anything consumable was shared with the faithful as a blessing. *Hint:* This is a nice piece of information for the food-beverage section.

SKILLS AND CAREERS Did this god/dess protect any particular group of people, like artists, bards, metalsmiths, and the like? If so, you can try and support that group mundanely and metaphysically by holding rituals or casting spells on their behalf. If you're really inspired, take up a new hobby (like weaving if your goddess was a weaver, or singing if your god protected vocalists)!

SYMBOLS Was this god/dess associated with a particular symbol or emblem? The predominant type of symbol for most world deities is geometric (circle, square, diamond, triangle, etc.). For example, Arianrhod in Celtic tradition is represented by a wheel (circle) because she's associated with the cycle of life-death-rebirth. *Hint:* Copy this association into the symbol section of your Book of Shadows. Meditate on what that symbolism indicates about the god/dess' personality and powers.

TAROT CORRESPONDENCE If you like working with Tarot cards, it's interesting to see if a god/dess has become associated with any of the Major Arcana over time, and, if so, why. You may find this information very helpful in readings. *Hint:* Copy this idea into the fortune-telling section of your spellbook.

TOOLS OR GARB If this god/dess is shown in art or stories with specific types of tools or clothing, you may want to use these somehow in your ritual work. For example, if the god bears a sword, this might be a good choice as your "athame." *Hint:* Note this option under tools in your spellbook.

FESTIVAL DAYS Most popular god/desses have festival dates when people gathered to honor that power, or dates when they were considered part of the observance. You will want to do something special for your selected god/dess on these days, so it helps to have historical details in your Book of Shadows to use as helpmates in creating your own observance. *Hint:* Keep a list of these holidays in the Wheel of Life section of your book.

OTHER CORRESPONDENCES (astrological, color, numerological) Any other bits of information you gather to round out this Divine persona will help you later in designing any mystical procedure in which he or she will be involved. For example, if a god/dess is associated with a particular astrological sign or lunar phase, you might want to invoke his or her assistance when the Moon is in that sign or phase. *Hint:* You may also want to add any associations you discover into the Wheel of Life section of your book.

Honoring and Communing With the Divine

With all that information gathered, the next step is finding meaningful ways to bring this power into your everyday life. Here's a list of ideas from my Book of Shadows that you can review. Feel free to take anything you find useful here and add it to your spellbook's pages.

- Highlight your home or sacred space with colors that represent the god/dess.
- Put an image that represents the god/dess on your altar (or at least use a candle that you can light to symbolize his or her presence).
- Use herbs and aromatics on yourself, around your home, and in the sacred space that are suited to that god/dess and his or her attributes.
- Add any symbols associated with the god/dess into your ritual clothing, altar cloths, nearby art, carve them into spell candles, etc. *Hint:* Cross-reference this last idea in the spellcraft section of your book.
- Leave offerings for this god/dess out regularly, especially outdoors where the animals can take your gift and put it to good use.
- Eat foods and drink beverages that the god/dess holds sacred in order to internalize their attributes. Also use these as postritual foods, or ritual libations. It's even nicer if some of the foods and beverages originate in the god/dess' culture. *Hint:* Copy this idea into the food-beverage section of your spellbook.
- Invite the god/dess into as many different magical procedures as possible. The more that deity is present, the greater rapport you'll establish.
- Meditate on various artistic renditions of this being, or descriptions you find in stories to give him or her fuller dimension.
- Pray and talk to the god/dess regularly in any way that feels right. *Hint:* Add prayers that you really like into that section of your spellbook.
- Find sacred music that somehow reminds you of the god/dess or mentions him or her by name, and play it often.

The World's Gods and Goddesses

The number of gods and goddesses in the world is overwhelming, so it was very difficult to determine which ones to include in this book. In thinking it over, I decided that a brief review of some deities directly associated with magic and spellcraft would be a good choice, since these beings can give you guidance and focus for working on your magical Book of Shadows! (Read other god and goddess guides if you'd like more information.)

God/dess and Country	Characteristics and Powers
Adonai Aretz (Israel)	God of magical manifestation through will.
Agizan (Voodoo)	God of psychic magic.
Artemis (Greece)	Goddess of all magical matters.
Brigit (Ireland)	Goddess of the occult, witches, and prophesy.
Dactyls (Greece)	Spirits who empower magical symbols. *Hint:* Cross-reference this information in the symbols section of your book.
Dakini (Buddhism)	Beings who govern magical initiation and spiritual insight.
Ea (Babylon)	God of incantations. *Hint:* Cross-reference this in the spellcraft section.
Freya (Norse)	Goddess of magic, good fortune, future-telling, and astuteness. *Hint:* Cross-reference this with the divination section.
Hecate (Greece)	Patroness of witches and spellcraft.
Hephaestus (Greece)	God of metal and gem magic. *Hint:* Cross-reference this with gem/metal/mineral correspondences.
Kamrusepas (Hittite)	Goddess of spells and magical arts.

God/dess and Country	Characteristics and Powers
Lud (Wales)	God of healing magic.
Ningirama (Mesopotamia)	God of magic and protection (snakes).
Pancaraksa (Buddhist)	Goddesses of spellcraft and magic formulas.
Re (Phoenician)	Goddess of moon magic.
Surya (Hindu)	God of Sun magic.
Thoth (Egypt)	God of ritual magic.

Applications

By definition, the god/dess can be anywhere, anytime. These Powers are not limited by our ideas of time and space, nor are they constrained by human expectations. For the divine to fill its function in the universe, it must be all things to all people, which certainly explains why there are so many images of the god/dess in the world. Even with this diversity, we can see that each god/dess fulfills a function; each has a face, name, and characteristics to which some humans can relate and aspire. They are, in effect, a mirror reflecting what enlightenment can be for the human soul.

So how does this affect the way we weave our magic and how we walk the Wiccan path? I can't speak for anyone else, but for me it shapes my magical methods dramatically. I release my spells into wiser hands than my own for care and direction. I raise power augmented by that Source. And I live my life feeling, deep within, that I will eventually reunite with that Source in one form or another through reincarnation. In other words, for me, the god/dess *is* my magic, and therefore there is no limit to the way that Source can be used, as long as I do so respectfully.

I say all this because it's not my job, nor my right, to tell you how to work with the Divine, or how to express your relationship with the Sacred in your magic. You'll have to figure that one out for yourself, and it's a great topic for consideration in your Magical Diary.

Suggested Reading

Witch's God. Janet and Stewart Farrar. Custer, Wash.: Phoenix, 1989.

Witch's Goddesses. Janet and Stewart Farrar. Custer, Wash.: Phoenix, 1987.

Encyclopedia of Gods. Michael Jordan. New York: Facts on File, 1993.

Guide to the Gods. Marjorie Leach. Santa Barbara, Calif.: ABC Clio, 1997.

Personal Notes

PART III

Your Magical Diary

U p until now your Book of Shadows has focused on methods, processes, correspondences—basically the technicalities of magic. Your Magical Diary, however, deals with *you:* your heart, your vision, your spiritual growth. Really, a Book of Shadows would be totally incomplete without a section like this one because you are your magic. It's really that simple.

For those of you who work regularly with a computer, this part of your spellbook is perfectly suited to electronic preparation. Since your Magical Diary will always be growing and expanding, having it on the computer will allow you to reorder, organize, and keep things where they belong. You can always print this section out periodically so you have an actual paper copy to which to refer. If you decide to take this route, however, *please* back up your Magical Diary onto a disk at least once a month (or make paper copies, or both). There's nothing more heartbreaking than to have a system crash that leaves all your treasures inaccessible or fragmented.

For the Magical Diary part of your spellbook, I'm suggesting seven different sections or files, seven being the number of completion. It is also a lunar number with strong associations to both the will and the intuitive self, which are both so important to magic. The sections I'm suggesting here include:

- Notable and Quotable
- Lecture and Lesson Notes
- Networking
- Dream Diary

- Insights and Introspection
- Magical Commitments and Goals
- Personal Magic: Success and failure

As with the rest of your Book of Shadows, you can use these divisions as they stand or come up with personal ones more suited to your path and life. For example, you might want to have some notes on sacred sites you've visited, or a section that has photographs of people and events that have affected you deeply. In any case, follow the same thoughtful process as you have up to this point and the resulting Book of Shadows will meet or exceed all your expectations.

14

Notable and Quotable

This part of your spellbook should house any inspiring bits of text, speeches, music, poetry, or whatever, that strike a deep emotional chord within you. Make sure you note the source of an item so you can return to it at a later date, and copy it carefully so as to maintain the original form.

Here are some of the quotes I keep handy. You'll notice I've subdivided them by theme. Why? So they're handy for magic, of course! Sometimes I use them as part of incantations, other times as part of rituals, and other times still as teaching tools. These verses also make a good meditative focus.

BEAUTY

The fountain of beauty is the heart.   —Francis Quarles

DESTINY

The acts of this life are the destiny of the next.   —Old Eastern proverb

EARTH

Love the world as you love yourself, then can you care for all things. —Lao Tzu, *Tao Te Ching*

My book is the nature of created things, and any time I wish to read the words of God, the book is before me.   —Anthony of the Desert

Nature and wisdom always say the same. —Juvenal

FAITH

Faith is a certain image of eternity. —Jeremy Taylor

Faith is the pencil of the soul. —T. Burbridge

FORTUNE (Fate)

The wheel of fortune turns round incessantly. —Confucius

GOD

To grasp God in all things, this is the sign of your new birth. —Meister Eckhart

The great spirit is the life that is in all things. —Rolling Thunder

In the beginning, God shattered like a giant crystal. One small shard landed in every human soul. So, we are forever seeking to reunite with each other and God to be whole. —My friend Barb

HUMOR

Good humor is the health of the soul. —Stanislaus

LIFE

You must live in the present, launch yourself on every wave, find eternity in the moment. —Henry David Thoreau

LOVE

There were three, you and I and we. Without you I would be less than one. —Leonard Nimoy, *You and I*

If you love it enough, anything will talk to you. —George Washington Carver

SELF

When you look inside yourself you see the universe and all the stars in infinity. —Carl Jung

Suggested Reading

Spiritual Literacy. Federic Brussat and Mary Ann Brussat. New York: Scribner, 1996.

Any version of *Bartlett's Familiar Quotations.*

Personal Notes

15

Lecture and Lesson Notes

Even if you're a solitary witch, walking the path of magic brings you across other spiritually-minded people or groups. As you have these encounters, you're likely to discover individuals from magical "schools" that are different from your own (like shamanism, Dianic Witches, Gardinarians, or whatever), but whose ideas are quite helpful in your magical practice. So, this section of your Diary and Spellbook will be dedicated to the lessons you learn from these people, and from speakers you may hear when you attend Wiccan and Pagan gatherings, lectures, and workshops.

In assembling these notes, you might want to think about including any or all of the following:

• The date, time, and place where you got the information. This will help you know which gatherings are the most empowering and inspirational for you. *Hint:* You might want to cross-reference these events in the Wheel of Life section. You may also notice a pattern here that indicates when you personally are more open and receptive to teaching.

• Who you got the information from. This person may be someone to whom you can turn again and again for insights. Or, it may be someone whose name you can give to another seeker as a good resource.

• The information itself. This will likely be the largest, or second largest, part of the entry.

• How the whole experience affected you. This will not only increase your appreciation of the notes, but help encourage internalization of the most important points. Consider: Do you think about the subject differently now? If so, how? Will you be changing any of your magical practices or personal habits because of what you've learned? If so, why?

In reading the above list, you might get the mistaken impression that lessons have to be lengthy, which isn't the case at all. There are times that I've had one word or short phrase entries in this part of my Book of Shadows—words that I want to reflect upon later, like:

> Be-ing
> The Magic is ME
> Life is a ritual
> Live presently

Each of these words and phrases is a meditation unto itself. *Hint:* Add the results of meditating on words and phrases like these into either the introspection section of your diary or the meditation section of your Book of Shadows. They are sentences I heard in passing that lodged in my heart and soul like an arrow. So, don't worry about how long or short your lessons appear to anyone else. What's important here is the quality of learning, not the quantity of writing. Along the same lines, bear in mind that your lecture and lesson notes need not make sense to anyone but you. This is, after all, *your* Book of Shadows.

Personal Notes

16

Networking

Because many members of the magical community have remained in the figurative "broom closet" out of necessity, we often find ourselves having to dig and search for other Witches, Pagans, and like-minded people. Be that as it may, the magical community has one of the most powerful, fast networks I have ever seen, especially now that the Internet has come into our hands. And what do we do with this network? A lot!

When there's a need in the community, it gets communicated through these lines. When someone wants to find out important information, people help them find it through our networks. When someone is looking for a coven to join, ritual tools, healers, other goods, or spiritual services, all these requests and many more are carried on the magical web that's been carefully knitted over the years, and extended to every corner of the globe.

With this in mind, this section of your Magical Diary will list the individuals and groups who are part of your personal web. Consider this a kind of detailed address book, if you will, that lists any, or all, of the following information:

Person or group's name.
Name by which they prefer to be called (in and out of the circle): There are some folks in the magical community whose real names

I still don't know after fourteen years, simply because those people are more comfortable with a chosen magical name. Always respect this choice. *Hint:* You may want to add a section on names and their meaning into your Book of Shadows. There's a lot of power in names, and you can learn to use them as tools for personal growth.

Address: Be sure to note if you can give this information out to a fellow seeker without first getting permission from the person or group.

Phone number, E-mail, and fax: See Address for guidelines regarding sharing contact information.

Magical areas of expertise: If you're going to network, it's a lot easier if you know where to begin. If you have a friend who studies folklore and another who is a Cabbalist, their ability to help with a specific question is going to vary. Noting the person or group's area of expertise provides a starting point for the networking process. It will help you find the people whose knowledge matches your need and they can further extend the web if need be.

Affiliations: If a person has any alphabet soup before or after his or her name, and if he or she is a member of various groups that influence the magical community, note it here.

How or where you met them, and key words about the meeting: I can't tell you how many times this has saved me embarrassment when I come home from a large event and start getting E-mails from people. After I meet someone that I think I'll have contact with in the future, I make a note of their name and the core issues of our conversation. For example, if someone was looking for a coven to work with the note might say, "Mary—find Celtic-oriented coven." As soon as I get home this goes in my Magical Diary (which I happen to maintain on the computer) so I can refer back to it when letters, calls, or E-mail arrives.

Birthdate, hobbies, likes and dislikes: This is not essential information, but it's really nice to have handy for the folks that help you regularly. Send them a virtual birthday card or yule gift to say thanks.

Crash space: Does this person or group have houses or land where you can stay when you travel to that area of the country? If so, what arrangements need to be made ahead of time to secure space? Pagans are, for the most part, friendly folk who don't mind sharing space with courteous people. It saves money, encourages fellowship, and fosters a more open exchange of ideas and information.

Other notes: This section is pretty open-ended. Include gatherings where you know you can see this person or group regularly, any projects they're working on (like getting Pagan land for gatherings), any "no-nos" like allergies to pets or specific foods (if you see them often), and so forth. *Hint:* Cross-reference the gathering information with the Wheel of Life section in your Book of Shadows.

In other words, fill out this section so you can communicate quickly and effectively, no matter the situation.

Personal Notes

17

Dream Diary

Keeping a dream diary is something I highly recommend to any spiritually-minded person. While we sleep, even science agrees that we're able to receive messages from our own minds more easily, and integrate much of what happens to us during the day. By extension, this means that our dreams may represent one of the best mediums through which the Divine, spirit guides, animal teachers, and other spiritual entities can also reach out to us, teach us, and guide our path. Note, however, that *both* the information you get from your self, and that which comes from outside your self, is important to a Magical Diary. You are the principle force in your life for creating positive magic, therefore you are among your own best teachers!

I know some people reading this will say: "But I don't dream, so how can I keep a dream diary as part of my Book of Shadows?" Actually, you do dream, you just don't *remember* them. So, I'd like to digress for just a moment and provide a few hints that will help people in this regard. What I suggest is sipping a warm cup of jasmine tea before bed, and making yourself a sachet filled with rose petals, marigolds, and mugwort, and placing it under your pillow. Then, as you go to sleep try an affirmation like, "I will dream and remember." Or, perhaps pray to Spirit for assistance. See what happens with time and diligence!

For those who have no trouble remembering dreams, and those who eventually teach themselves to remember them, the next question becomes exactly what to record about the dream in your Magical Diary. What I find works best is to tape record or write down the dream immediately upon waking. A little later I return to those notes and review them, looking for anything that may have been caused by the news and entertainment media, situations in my day, my sleeping environment, fantasies, or a bad choice of presleep food! Generally I don't include these things in my dream journal, feeling that they're less likely to house spiritual messages. Even so, if you're not sure, then keep all the information.

I also recommend waiting about twenty-four hours before transferring anything into your permanent dream diary. During the day, you may get flashes or clearer memories of the dream that are important to its meaning. You'll want to include these in the correct sequence of events, not as "add-ons."

After transferring your dream's content into the diary, make notes about what you feel the dream means. You can use a dream key to help you like *Language of Dreams* (Freedom, CA: Crossing Press, 1997), but you must also trust your instincts here. Dream interpretation is a highly subjective art, but there are some simple guidelines that will help you better understand your dreams. *Hint:* If you create a dream key for your Book of Shadows, you may want to copy these guidelines into that section.

They are:

• Look for a theme. If, for example, you see a wall being demolished, a glass breaking, and a tree being cut down, the overall theme here is destruction or waste. So, the next question becomes—what is it that you feel is being destroyed or wasted?

• Trust your first response or gut instincts. If you have an immediate emotional or mental response to the dream, it will usually prove to be accurate.

• Accept the possibility that there may be instances of precognition, postcognition, or past lives expressing themselves through your dream. If you can't find any meaning in a dream and it seems particularly realistic, this may be why.

• Recognize the obvious. Don't go hunting for some deep, hidden meaning to a dream when the lesson is staring you in the face. Truthfully, our mind is rarely enigmatic—it usually tells it like it is, in a form we can accept. If that form, for you, is symbolic, then that's the way your mind and Spirit will communicate. All that remains is finding the value in those symbols (which you can explore using information from the symbolism section in your Book of Shadows).

• Avoid performing any type of dream interpretation when you're sick, tired, angry, or gloomy. No matter how positive the dream's imagery may be, these mental and physical states tend to accent the negatives and you'll draw the wrong conclusions.

• Realize that some dreams won't make sense right away, so leave ample space beneath the entry. This is what I call a "trigger dream"—something over the next few hours, days, or weeks will activate the meaning in the dream, and make it clear to you. That's when you'll want to return to the diary and finish the entry.

Personal Notes

18

Insights and Introspection

Of all parts of your Magical Diary, this one will have the most "diarylike" look and feel to it. It's also the section that often reveals your spiritual progress most intimately. Exactly how you handle this part of the diary is really up to you, but here are some ideas worth considering:

Daily Reflections

When you get up in the morning or before you go to bed, write for a few minutes. What do you hope to achieve personally and spiritually today? What things bothered you during the day and why? How do you want to handle these things tomorrow? See, I told you it's just like a normal diary but with spiritual overtones! Like it or not, everyday life affects your spiritual pursuits, so one cannot (and should not) be separated from the other.

Meditation and Visualization Notes

Many people use meditation and visualization as a way of improving personal comprehension and perspective. So, when you have a particularly poignant experience, your insights about it should be added into the diary. Otherwise, you may simply want

221

to note the success or failure of the meditation in that portion of your spellbook.

Ritual Notes

Some rituals go smoothly, others do not. Some raise an amazing amount of power that transforms everyone present, others do not. So, after you've attended a ritual it is often helpful to make notes about what went right or wrong, what you liked or disliked (and why), and what portions held the greatest amount of meaning for you. These notes will prove *very* helpful in the future should you ever wish to design your own rituals, or if you want to perform the ritual again upon making suitable changes for greater success.

Divination Notes

If you get readings or do them for yourself, it's very important to keep notes about them. Even though the reading is likely to make sense right now, you will often find that it has another meaning altogether in the future. So, when you create this section of your diary, leave room for future reflections too—the new dimensions to the reading that life, experience, new people, or circumstances illuminate.

Random Observations

Once you begin practicing magic, you'll find that ideas about various magical procedures and philosophies will come to you at the oddest times, triggered by unexpected things. So, carry a small notebook with you everywhere possible and make note of those observations as they come. Then, once a week or so, review the notes and see which ones you'd like to keep in this portion of your diary, and transfer them accordingly. As you do, don't overlook the opportunity to add a little more substance if the observation motivates and inspires it. And, leave plenty of room for later additions or reflections too!

Birthday Writings

Each year on my birthday I spend a little time musing about the previous year, what I accomplished, and where I'm hoping to go in the days ahead. The following year, I re-read all the previous entries, then add a new one. Believe me when I say you'll find these entries to be very insightful. They'll teach you much about yourself, your dreams, your accomplishments, and the like that might otherwise go unnoticed.

Holiday Writings

What does each juncture on the Wheel of Life mean to you? Does this change from year to year, mirroring the changes you're experiencing within? Writing in your journal about a holiday as it's happening helps internalize the energies of that observance, and really brings the meaning home to your heart and life. Don't forget to make notes of celebratory activities that you found particularly empowering so you can use them again.

Nature Notes

Whenever you get the chance to listen to the earth's voice, I strongly advocate it. Nature is an important teacher. She whispers to us in every wind, the crackle of leaves, the cry of birds, and the pitter-patter of paws across the forest lawn. Even if that "forest" is only a nearby park, take your diary out with you and make notes of the impressions you get from Earth's classroom.

Really, there's no limit to exactly what you can write in this part of your diary. It's the intimate reflections of everything that's going on in, and around, your life on all levels (mental, physical, and spiritual). Do, however, make time to read this over regularly so it can become a tool for self-actualization and change.

Personal Notes

_____

_____

_____

_____

_____

_____

_____

_____

_____

_____

_____

_____

_____

_____

_____

_____

_____

19

Magical Commitments and Goals

Any time you make a promise to yourself or the universe, detail it in your Magical Diary. Then, keep track of your progress in achieving your goal. As you do, pay particular attention to and note any or all of the following:

The Exact Commitment or Goal

What did you decide to try to do, and when? Was the timing significant, and if so why? What motivated this decision? What do you hope to accomplish at the very least? If this exercise were to manifest in ideal form, what would be the outcome? The usefulness of these notes will become clear later as your efforts bring you closer to completion.

Feeling Held Back or Stumbling Blocks

You'll want to design magical procedures to release those constraints and tear down the walls. *Hint:* If this procedure proves effective and helpful, copy it into the appropriate section of your Book of Shadows.

Follow up this magic with concrete efforts that will support the energy and give the universe a chance to step in with aid.

> *Important:* Never work any magic that you're not willing to support through honest, mundane efforts. The universe is willing to meet us halfway, but we have to go the other half in order for the journey to have the greatest meaning and results.

Helpful and Motivating Forces

Return to these again and again until you attain your goal or fulfill your commitment. If the help or motivation comes from a person, ask if it's okay to come to them (don't simply assume help will be given). Remember, this is *your* spiritual quest, not theirs, and you must be the guru for your own life. Don't let outside assistance become a crutch or the entire exercise will suffer.

Personal Struggles

The inner conflicts that often occur when you're trying to reach a spiritual plateau are tremendous teachers. They'll reveal both your weaknesses, which you can always work on, and your strengths, which you'll want to depend on!

External and Internal Manifestations

While you're trying to reach a particular goal or fulfill a commitment, I can almost guarantee the process will bring about changes in your life, either within or without (and often both). These transformations are a very important reflection of your spiritual learning process, so they should be given ample space in your Magical Diary.

Results

When all is said and done, what was the outcome of this effort? Are you pleased with the results, and why? Would you recommend this as something for another person to try, and if so how much magical knowledge is necessary to succeed? Do you plan to repeat the effort, and if so when and why?

Add anything else to your notes that you feel was significant to your success or failure, then use that knowledge in considering future goals and commitments.

Personal Notes

20

Personal Magic: Success and Failure

Next to personal observations about your entire spiritual life, I think you will find this one of the most important and useful sections in your Magical Diary. Here you will be making notes of any personally created spell, ritual, meditation, or other construct, and its results. As you make these notes, be sure to include any or all of the following information:

If the Procedure Was Based on Another Source

If it was, what was the source and how did you change the procedure? Also *why* did you make changes? Sometimes this information is even more important than the details since it can reveal if there are certain things about a magical procedure that you are (or are not) comfortable with.

The Exact Details of the Procedure

These include the components you used, the atmosphere you created, the wording or movements, etc. If the procedure is very effective, you'll want to use it again, so these notes will help you recreate the whole process perfectly. If the procedure doesn't seem to work, the details here will help you determine what needs to be changed.

When You Tried the Procedure

In the Wheel of Life section of your Book of Shadows, we detailed timing and its usefulness to magic. If the timing you used for this process proved helpful, you'll want to note it for future reference.

The Conditions Under Which the Procedure Took Place

Was it raining? Was there a lot of noise outside your home? Were you tired, energetic, happy, sad, expectant, or curious? All these things can (and often do) affect your magic. So, if the conditions weren't perfect, and the process doesn't work quite right, you can always try again when circumstances are more favorable.

It's not wise to judge the effectiveness of a self-created magical procedure based on one attempt. I usually suggest three tries, each of which is done under slightly different conditions. If after the third try it's still not working, then you probably need to rethink the details.

Account Anything Unusual That Happened During the Procedure

In other words if you suddenly changed a component or action based on a direction from Spirit, note it! Or, if something makes you uncomfortable, note that too. Even though you know yourself pretty well, we can never be totally sure of how any magical process will feel and flow until it's actually tried (that's because of the energies created). In either case, heeding a direction from Spirit will leave you with a more effective, meaningful procedure to refer to in the future. Notes of any feelings of unease will help you eliminate factors that, for whatever reason, don't help your magic.

The Results

You will likely need to leave a space for this in your diary, since most magic doesn't manifest immediately. Give the spell, ritual, or whatever plenty of time to show signs of working, then return to this spot and make your assessment.

Personal Notes

Afterword: Using Your Book of Shadows

After having gone to all the effort of assembling this spellbook, you certainly don't want to just leave it on a shelf somewhere collecting dust! Use it every day like a good cookbook to put together the best ingredients for living a positive magical life. With that in mind, I'd like to leave you with these parting thoughts:

- Know yourself and your magical art and live accordingly.
- Balance, vision, and personalization are three keys to a fulfilling life and powerful magic.
- There is no "right way" or "wrong way" to achieve enlightenment. What's most important is that your spiritual path (or that of someone else) helps you live fully, happily, and makes you the best person you can be.
- Never stop learning or growing, and allow your magic to grow with you. A belief system that never changes dies, or worse, becomes a rote liturgy without meaning or power.
- Internalize and apply your spiritual magical knowledge every day so that you become a living ritual, and each day becomes an act of worship.

- *Be* the magic, in word and in deed. Celebrate the wonder in each moment as a miracle, and as an opportunity to weave magic into every corner of your reality.

If you're looking for ritual tools, herbs, robes, and other magical gear, may I suggest first looking to any New Age shops in your area, health food cooperatives, botanical shops, the Internet, and even perhaps mail-order catalogs that come your way. My only caution is to try and find outlets with an established reputation for service. For example, if you're looking for other books about any of the topics herein, I suggest www.amazon.com. They're fantastic, and very well rounded.

Nice athames (ritual knives) can be purchased at any cutlery store, and even sometimes at secondhand stores. Likewise, Good Will or Salvation Army stores often have clothes that are beautiful and affordable if you want to buy something special to wear in circle. Secondhand stores often have other magic tools such as incense burners, altar cloths, and candle holders. Remember, there's no rule that says magical gear has to be expensive. If you can make it yourself, or find it at a garage sale, all the better! Making an item saturates it with personal energy, and finding items is a neat way to recycle.

My best wishes are with you in this wonderful adventure.

About the Author

Trish Telesco is thirty-eight years old, the mother of three, wife of fourteen years, chief human to five pets, and a professional author with more than thirty metaphysical books on the market. These include *The Herbal Arts* (Citadel Press), *Goddess in My Pocket, The Language of Dreams, Kitchen Witch's Cookbook*, and other diverse titles.

Trish travels at least once a month to give lectures and workshops around the country. She has appeared on several television segments including one for the syndicated show *Sightings* on multicultural divination systems, and one for the *Debra Duncan Show* on modern Wicca. In addition, Trish maintains a strong, visible presence in metaphysical journals including *Circle Network News, Silver Chalice*, and *Aquarius*, and on the Internet (www.pce.net/ptelesco).

Trish considers herself a down-to-earth Kitchen Witch. She was originally self-trained and self-initiated, but later received initiation into the Strega tradition of Italy, which gives form and fullness to the folk magic Trish practices in everyday life. She believes strongly in following personal vision, being tolerant of other traditions, making life an act of worship, and being creative so that magic grows with you. In effect, Trish ascribes to the KISS ("Keep It Simple, and Sublime") school of magic, and has practiced as a solitary for over fourteen years now. Her hobbies include gardening, herbalism, brewing, singing, handcrafts, antique restoration, and landscaping.